AF241836

THE BANNONBRIDGE MUSICIANS

OTHER BOOKS BY RAYMOND FRASER

fiction
Bliss
The Madness Of Youth
Repentance Vale
The Trials Of Brother Bell
In Another Life
The Grumpy Man
In A Cloud Of Dust And Smoke
Costa Blanca
Rum River
The Struggle Outside
The Black Horse Tavern

memoirs, essays & stories
When The Earth Was Flat

biography
Todd Matchett: Confessions of a Young Criminal
The Fighting Fisherman: The Life Of Yvon Durelle

poetry
Before You're A Stranger
Macbride Poems
The More I Live
I've Laughed And Sung
Waiting For God's Angel
Poems for the Mirimichi

THE BANNONBRIDGE MUSICIANS

revised edition

Raymond Fraser

Lion's Head Press

© Copyright 1978, 2014 Raymond Fraser

All rights reserved. No reproduction is permitted without prior written permission from the publisher except for brief passages in reviews. Requests for photocopying or other reprographic copying may be directed to Access Copyright.

The Bannonbridge Musicians was originally published by Breakwater Books in 1978. This 3rd edition has been revised and edited by the author, and stands as the definitive version.

Cover painting by Vincent Van Gogh

Library and Archives Canada Cataloguing in Publication

Fraser, Raymond, 1941-, author
The Bannonbridge musicians / Raymond Fraser. --
Revised edition.

First published: Portugal Cove, Nfld. : Breakwater Books, c1978.
ISBN 978-1-928020-03-5 (pbk.)

I. Title.

PS8561.R3B36 2014   C813'.54   C2014-906089-0

Lion's Head Press
Toronto • Canada

PART ONE

IT WAS 1961, THE YEAR Sully got killed. We were on our way around the world that summer, Toronto, Vancouver, San Francisco, Mexico, Caracas, Dakar, Casablanca, Barcelona, Paris, Rome, Athens, Cairo — But first stopping off at Toronto to get jobs and save enough money to finance the trip. After more than a month there we were surviving on dry toast and tea — that's all we could afford to eat. Our room was on Jarvis Street, on the top floor of an old soot-blackened brick house with a front yard full of weeds. Because of the look of the house our room surprised us, when we first saw it; it was bright, clean and spacious, and the rent was only eight dollars a week. We paid the first two weeks, but not the last four. It was all trust and generosity on the part of our landlord, who was everything landlords aren't supposed to be, while we were the worst kind of tenants. He took us at our word that we'd find work and pay the rent, and in the end let us sneak off in the night. He was an eastern European of some sort, Polish maybe, with a name full of z's and x's and c's, and a profound sadness in his eyes. We never found out anything about him, he lived a few doors down the street from his rooming house, and when we fell behind in our rent we kept clear of him. When we did run into him he never said a word about the rent. We told him we were still looking for work. The sadness in his eyes made me feel guilty, a little.

There was a janitor in our building, a Newfie by the name of Kearns who looked like the Hunchback of Notre Dame without the hump — an ape-like cross-eyed character with a crazed scowl on his face. As was typical at that address he was drunk more often than not. He used to get the passions for Cookie, who lived on the second floor in the room directly beneath ours. Different nights we'd hear him lurch up the stairs from his basement room and start hammering on her door. In a thick-tongued voice he'd shout, "Is you in, Cookie? Cookie, is you in? Open the door! I wants to see you! Cookie, is you in? Is you in there, Cookie?"

He'd get no response, but all the same he'd stand there for a good half hour beating on the door and hollering. You could hear his voice thundering through the building.

"Cookie, is you in? I wants to see you! Let me in, Cookie! It's me! Is you in there?"

You'd swear her room was empty, for all the reaction he got; but he knew when she was there. Usually after a time we'd hear her voice call out through the door, "Go away and leave me alone!" That's all she'd say, but the fact she said anything at all encouraged him.

"Is that you, Cookie? I wants to see you! I knows you're in there! Open the door, Cookie, let me in! I only wants to talk to you!"

It got on your nerves. After a long time he'd stomp off, muttering drunkenly, only to return in a few minutes and start all over again. "It's me, Cookie! I'se got something I wants to tell you! Is you there, Cookie? Open the door!"

Just to look at the man in broad daylight was unnerving. Those nights when he was ranting around we kept our door locked and talked in whispers, afraid he'd change course and come up and murder us — to relieve his frustrations.

"If that crazy bastard don't kill us we'll starve to death," said Sully.

Our hunger made us apprehensive. We talked about making tracks. The landlord had to run out of tolerance, despite his good-heartedness. Luckily he never looked into our room; it was a shambles, a dump, mostly because of the newspapers. We used to get them from the open boxes on the streets, pretending to drop a dime into the slot. Every day we got The Globe & Mail, The Star, The Telegram, and scanned the Help Wanted ads. We knew what we were after.

Sailing yacht cruising tomorrow for the Caribbean urgently requires two young deckhands, experience not necessary. New Brunswick natives preferred. Must be able to hold their liquor and willing to entertain millionaire owner's two beautiful and debauched teenaged daughters; excellent salary.

Once we'd read through the papers they got tossed aside and left where they landed, so that after five weeks there was a carpet of them a foot deep, from wall to wall. Then there were bottles — wine bottles, rum bottles, gin bottles — the beer bottles all returned for the deposit — and tin cans, and cigarette packages, and bags of garbage. It was a terrible mess — you could hardly get into the room.

Our finances had shrunk to the point where we had thirty-five cents between us, and we were getting weaker and more indolent than usual from our tea-and-toast diet. We'd given up our plans of roaming the world, and had decided to return home — All we had to do was get around to it. We found it hard to break our habit of staying up all night and playing cards, drinking tea, eating toast, talking about one thing and another — and then sleeping from dawn until mid-afternoon, at which time it was too late in the day to set out hitchhiking a thousand miles. What we were after was an early morning start, get away while the landlord was still in bed asleep, but when we'd been awake the whole night all we felt like doing was hitting the sack.

It was nine o'clock in the evening and I'd gone down to the second floor where the building's only toilet was located, and I was just starting up the stairs again when Cookie's door opened and she peered out at me. "Come here, doll. Come here, I want to see you."

We knew Cookie quite well by this time; different occasions she'd asked us in for a drink. She was always at the bottle, every day, never a day off. We used to see her from our window setting out in the afternoon for the wine store, dancing along on her tiptoes, waving her arms and sailing up the street as though there was music in her ears. She was in her late fifties – quite a dilapidated old thing– but she tried to keep up her appearance as best she could. Her hair was bleached, her face thickly powdered, her cheeks rouged and her fingernails polished scarlet.

"Have a drink with me, doll. I don't want to drink alone. I've got some wine. Come into my room, doll." Judging by her glassy eyes and the slur of her voice she'd been doing well enough on her own so far. I said I wouldn't mind a drop.

"Sit down, doll. Where's your friend?" Her room was smaller than ours but with the same essential furniture: bed, small table, chest of drawers with mirror, two chairs, a hotplate. The bed was low to the floor and unmade and Cookie eased herself carefully down onto it and sat there with her hands clasped primly in her lap.

"Where's your friend? Where's Sully? I haven't seen Sully at all today."

"He's upstairs."

"Go and get him, doll. Bring him down and we'll all have a drink together. I like your friend."

"Okay."

I left her and went upstairs and found Sullivan lying on the bed with his nose in a newspaper, going through the Used Car ads. He was quite the sight, stretched out with his grimy bare feet crossed and his shirt off and his face fuzzied with the beard he was trying to grow. The picture of a holed-up con – a fugitive from the chain gang –

"Cookie's invited us for a drink," I said.

Without taking his eyes off the paper he said, "Yeah? Not again."

"Why, did she already ask you?"

"I can't stand that old whore, always trying to drag you into her room. I don't want to have to listen to her."

"Plug your ears. Come on, let's go."

"Naw, I don't want no wine."

"Are you sick?" I stared at him, amazed. "When did you ever turn down a drink before?"

"Listen to this. Fifty-three Pontiac, good condition, only two hundred bucks—"

"Never mind that. Come on."

"We should've bought one when we had the money, when we first come up. We could've got an old heap for a hundred-fifty, two hundred bucks—"

"We should've done a lot of things."

"And got out of this hole, took off for Mexico, we'd be there right now. Just think—"

"Come on, Sully. What are you stalling for?"

"I'm not stalling."

"Well let's go downstairs and get at the grapes. She'll have it all drunk."

"Naw. You go, I don't feel like it."

"She's got smokes. There's a pack open on her table."

When we had money Sullivan was accustomed to smoking two large packs a day. When we started to go broke he switched to rolling his own until the time came when he couldn't even afford a package of tobacco. So then he took to rummaging about in the garbage bags for old butts which he broke apart and used the tobacco to roll further cigarettes out of – and then he made still more cigarets out of these butts, and so on, until there wasn't a grain of tobacco to be found in the room.

12

He laid the paper aside, considered a moment, then sat up and said, "Okay, I need a nail real bad. Only I ain't staying long."

When we went downstairs Cookie's door was open but she wasn't in her room. We went in anyway and took a chair. There were three water glasses full of wine on the table along with a bottle that was half full. On the floor beside the table there was an empty bottle.

"She must be in the can."

Sullivan's eyes immediately lit on the pack of cigarets. He picked it up, removed two and put them in his shirt pocket and replaced the package.

"She'll never miss those."

A minute or so later Cookie waltzed unsteadily through the door and said in her husky, slightly nasal voice, "Hello, my boys, it's so good you came to visit me. I'm always happy when you come to visit me." She smiled, showing her long divided yellow teeth. "Have a drink. I poured you both a drink. And have a cigarette. I'm so happy to see my boys."

With deliberation she moved around the table and sat on the bed, and we got into the wine. Out of the corner of my eye I saw Sullivan help himself to a cigarette and slip an extra one into his pocket.

"How are you, boys? How are you, Sully? I haven't seen you since... When was it you were here?"

"I'm all right, just fine," said Sullivan.

"And you..." She didn't remember my name. "How are you?" she said.

"Not too bad."

"And how are you, Sully? You're looking sweet. You were here yesterday, weren't you? We had a party, I think. I have a hard time remembering. Yesterday—"

"Nope, I wasn't here yesterday."

"No? I thought, doll—"

"You must've dreamt it, Cookie."

"Did I, doll?"

"You were probably drunk – imagining things." Sullivan gave me a sidelong look as if to say, "See, I told you she's crazy."

"I wasn't drunk, sweetheart. I've never been drunk in my whole life. I like to have a glass of wine every now and then but I never get drunk." She began to rock slowly back and forth on the bed. Her eyes fell on me. "Was it you? Were you here yesterday? Maybe it was you?"

"It wasn't me."

"No?"

"No, it must've been someone else."

"Yesterday... afternoon? Oh, I can't think too well today."

"I was over in the park yesterday afternoon – after I got up, I mean."

"Oh well. I'll figure it out later... How's everything, boys? How's life treating you?"

"Not bad."

"I'm glad to hear it." She paused a second, and said: "You know, boys, I get lonely here all alone. You want me to tell you something? Every night I lie in bed and I feel so lonely, and I just lie here waiting for my boys to come home and raise hell. I don't sleep well. No, I don't sleep well at all... I lie here and it's quiet and I think, pretty soon my boys will come home and

14

I won't be alone anymore. I hear you up there, singing and laughing and I know you're having a good time and that makes me feel better. It's like having company, I don't feel so lonely." She reached uncertainly for her glass and took a sip. "Light me a cigarette, doll."

Sullivan lit her one, at the same time slipping another one for himself into his pocket.

"Thank you, love. How's everything? Tell me, how are things going with the two of you?"

"Well... to tell you the truth, Cookie, not all that good," I said. "No money and no jobs and we're way behind in our rent."

She nodded understandingly.

"Gord was behind in his rent, him and Nan never paid no rent. Do you know Gord and Nan?"

Gord and Nan were a vagabond couple in their late thirties who had been living in the room next door to Cookie's.

"They're gone now," said Cookie.

"They are?"

"Yes, they left three nights ago. I miss Gord, him and Nan, they were nice to me. They were five weeks behind when they left. They gave the old man a pile of garbage to hold till they come back, they gave him a box of old clothes and broken dishes. It was just garbage. I'll tell you something, boys, they'll never come back, I know their kind. They don't want that garbage they left behind, they wouldn't have taken it with them anyway. That stuff's a dime a dozen. I know those kind of people, I know them, I've been around. They wait for the right time and before you know it they've run off. They tell the old man they'll pay him next week, every week they tell him that until finally he's glad to be rid of them. He's too soft, the old man. I always pay my rent, every week. I never get behind. But Gord and Nan, they wait till the right moment and then they leave, I've seen their kind before. A dime a dozen. Let me tell you something, Sully." She reached over and tapped him on the knee. The room was that small we were all within arm's reach of each other. "They won't be back. Do you know that?"

"I guess they won't," said Sullivan.

It wasn't long before our glasses were sitting empty on the table beside the wine bottle. Seeing this Cookie said, "Pour yourselves a drink, boys, help yourselves. I've got another quart in the closet."

I felt Sullivan's arm nudge me. He refilled the glasses. Being half-starved the way we were even one glass had quite a strong effect. It went straight to the head. I helped myself to a cigarette, even though at the time I didn't smoke too much.

"I miss Gord," Cookie said, rocking back and forth, her eyes bleary. "He used to come in with a bottle of wine and talk to me. But they won't be back. Nan said she didn't like this place and she wants to travel. When they make their money in Delhi with the tobacco they won't be back. That's where they went, they went up to Delhi to pick tobacco. After that they'll probably go down to the States or out West. If they ever come back to Toronto they'll get another place, they'll never pay the old man his rent... You know something, boys, I miss Gord. When he was here he used to throw that fellow from downstairs out. I hate that man. There's something wrong with him, he's mental."

"You mean the janitor?"

"He's not the janitor. He only thinks he is. He doesn't get paid, the old man gives him his room free for doing some odd jobs, it's only charity. There used to be a woman staying across the hall and he bothered her, he never stopped bothering her, always saying there was something wrong with the lights. Oh, he's sly. She left within a week. He comes to my room too but I put a spoon in the door. There's no lock so I have to put a spoon in it. He came up the other night and I told him I was resting. He tried to get in but he couldn't because I had a spoon in the door. It would take two men to open my door when it's locked like that. He's a dirty son of a bitch. He'd call the police if you ever took anything from one of the rooms..."

While she was rambling on my fingers played absently with the tinsel off the wine bottle top. I shaped a little hat out of it and put it on my head and looked in the mirror. Suddenly noticing me Cookie said, "You look cute, doll. It looks good on you. But it wouldn't look good on me, it's not my style. Let Sully try it, see how it looks on him."

"Go way, for Jesus sake. Don't be so simple." Sullivan swept my arm away as I tried to put the hat on his head.

"Tell me, boys, how's everything? How's it going with my boys?"

"Not so good," I repeated.

"Open that other bottle, Sully. It's in the closet. Do you see it there?"

"Yeah, here it is."

"Open it, doll. This one's almost finished. Have a cigarette. Was I dreaming about yesterday, lover? I can't think clearly today."

Her cigarettes were rapidly disappearing, due mainly to Sullivan pocketing them every chance he got. Before opening the new bottle he poured the remains of the old one into our glasses. Cookie took hers, which was full to the brim, and with a mechanical, seemingly unconscious movement picked it up and in one long drink drained it dry. For a minute she was still, sitting with her hands in her lap and her eyes distant and entranced. Then she shuddered. "A cigarette, doll," she said. I gave her one and held a match to it. "You're very kind to me," she said.

Normally Sullivan had a lot to say, but since we'd entered Cookie's room he'd hardly opened his mouth. Now he leaned towards me. "Why don't we shove off out of here tonight," he said out of the side of his mouth. "Pack our stuff and hit the road."

"What's that, Sully?" said Cookie.

"Nothing. I just said how great it was to have a drink for a change."

"Is that what you said? Have some more if you like. Anything for my boys."

"Tonight? You mean now?" I said to Sullivan, keeping my voice down.

"Sure, why not? We won't feel any better tomorrow."

He was right. We couldn't put it off forever, and in the glow of the wine the open road seemed inviting, now that I thought of it. Even in the black of night.

"All right. Let's go," I said.

"In a few minutes."

We spoke in undertones but it didn't much matter. After that great gulp of wine she'd taken, Cookie despite being only a few feet away was off in a world of her own, talking to herself.

"...that dirty son of a bitch, he went to the old man and told him we were having a party and the old man came over and told everyone to get out... They were my friends and we were just having a good time but that animal downstairs was jealous. I wouldn't let him in, I didn't want his ugly face around, so he told the landlord and everybody had to leave... They all left except old Joe. I like Joe. He was too stubborn. He lay on the bed and wouldn't move. The landlord left and Joe stayed... But we had a fight later and I haven't seen him since. But I'm going to surprise him. I'm going to get prettied up and visit Joe, he lives just down on Dundas, I know the place... that'll surprise him..."

"What Are we waiting for?" I said.

"Hold on a minute," said Sullivan.

"I like old Joe, he's a real gentleman when he's around me, but that filthy bastard downstairs, he should be in a zoo. I know what he's like. He wants to get my boys in trouble, he's jealous of everyone. He's jealous—" Her eyes made an attempt to focus on Sullivan—" He's jealous of you too, doll, he knows you came to see me yesterday, he knows we were drinking together, he knows what we were doing in here together, doll—"

I snorted. Sullivan's faced suddenly turned red as a beet. "You're nuts, Cookie, you're out of your goddamn mind."

"What's that, honey? Oh... I feel dizzy. I feel tired, boys..."

She rocked backwards and forwards, like a little girl, then reached for her empty glass and put it to her mouth, tipped it, looked curiously at it and put it back on the table.

"Don't laugh, you arsehole," Sullivan said to me. "I told you she's nuts."

"...there's something I should tell you boys, a lot of people don't know this but I don't have to pay for my room... Did you know that? I'll let you in on a secret... I'm an undercover agent for Eaton's. You didn't know that, boys... They give me all the money I want..."

"Let's get going," I said.

"Hang on, I told you. Don't be so impatient."

"I'll go and pack our stuff."

"Nossir, you're not leaving me alone with her."

"...I'll kill that man downstairs. You can't trust him, he'll get you thrown into the streets, he doesn't deserve to live... I'm going to kill him."

Sullivan took the remaining few cigarettes out of the pack and put them in his pocket with the others.

"...I got a sharp knife hid away and if it's the last thing I do I'll kill him. He's not going to hurt my boys... They come to me tired and it's not enough to comfort them, I have to get him. I'll get him with my knife... like this." She made a sleepy, half-hearted gesture. "Right in the spinal cord... It's dangerous but I'll do it and they won't catch me... You won't tell on me, will you, boys? My boys won't tell on me. He's out to get them but I'll kill him first. May God be with me..." Her head was nodding.

"Cookie, you better lie down and rest a while," said Sullivan.

"Eh? What did you say, doll? Pardon me... I didn't hear you."

"Lie down and rest for a while, why don't you?"

"Rest?"

"Sure. We'll stay here, and when you've had a rest we can drink some more."

"That's right, doll. Drink some more... You're right... All right, love, I'll just have a rest... I'm a little tired... Thank you, doll."

She stretched herself out on her back with her legs hanging over the side of the bed. "I'll kill him... revenge will be mine, I'll kill that man... son of a bitch... he won't hurt my boys..."

Sullivan looked at me and winked. Putting the cap back on the newly opened bottle of wine he tucked it in his belt and said, "Okay, let's haul arse." As we headed up the stairs to get our things ready he patted the bottle and said, "Just what the doctor ordered."

§

A week after we left Toronto Ralph Ramsay spotted us straggling into Bannonbridge, the heels and soles worn off our shoes, our unshaven faces smeared with sweat and dust, clothes stained from sleeping in fields and ditches... He didn't recognize us at first, took us for a couple of tramps passing through town, and almost walked by. He was on the other side of Water Street, his mind on other things. He'd just got his welfare cheque in the mail and was on his way to cash it before catching the train for Toronto (so he maintained later)... going over in his mind Sully's letter of a few weeks before describing the time we were having up there: the women, different ones every night, the booze cheap as tap water, our luxury apartment, great jobs available. He was ready, all set to make the break — it was now or never; friends waiting in the big city to receive him, give him a place to stay, find him the job of his dreams. There were plenty of ads for trumpet players, Sully wrote.

Then he did a double-take. Those bedraggled bums shuffling along the other side of the street, half dead with exhaustion and starvation – He told us later, what a close call it was—" If I'd missed you and gone up there alone – Holy sufferin'! All by myself in Toronto..." Shaking his head at his near fate. "And me thinking you were living like kings—"

§

My old man's way of living was enough to put me off work, at least while I could get away with it. He was at the job six days a week – always – work, eat and sleep, that was all he did, he had no time or energy for anything else; total self-sacrifice, slaving for $140 a month. He was the parish gravedigger and general handyman about the church, keeping the furnace going, cleaning the floors, the pews, mending the roof. Mowing the lawns in summer, raking leaves in the fall, shovelling snow in winter, planting the winter's dead in the spring.

There was a small college in Bannonbridge called St. Timothy's and with nothing better to do I signed up there for the coming year. It was cheap to go if you lived in town, less than $200 a year for tuition and books, the whole shot, and you didn't have to pay in advance. They weren't strict about it – you could wait till you were out in the world earning your fortune with your BA before giving them their money. I'd have free board at home, with only the old guy and myself there, the rest of the family dead or gone away. I'd be the housekeeper, the grocery shopper, the cook. A couple of more years and I could be a teacher, or go to the seminary and be a priest. All in all a great prospect! Preparing myself for something I didn't want to do. In a classroom when I wanted to be out seeing the world.

§

I was standing off by myself at the edge of the dance floor, regretting that I hadn't gone to the tavern instead and spent my seventy-five cents there; I could hardly hear myself think for the band – the amplifiers booming, electric guitars, volcanic sounds – stomach throbbing with the bass beat –

I hadn't got Corinne out of my mind, not entirely, but she wasn't at the dance, so I was spared the usual comedy routine. All the familiar faces, the same girls every week – I recognized them all – no happy surprises.

I could do without the ritual with Corinne. Walking up to her, where she sat with her girlfriends, like a door-to-door salesman selling cockroach powder or plastic dogshit for party jokes or somesuch – something like that – You could tell by the reaction –

"No, thank you." She wasn't having any. A mere instant to dismiss me, a stranger at the door. Smiling and chatting again with her friends.

"No, thank you."

"Okay. Fuck you." You had to say something — for your pride — Well, I didn't care really. It used to be different, but all good things come to an end. I was cold sober. The best thing to do was finish my cigarette and head for home. I was smoking regularly now, rolling my own. The old man had started leaving packages of Vogue and Player's around — At my age it was time to start smoking, he must have thought. He had a butt in his mouth from morning to night; it was his one and only extravagance.

I was on the point of making for the door when Sully materialized out of the crowd, drifting unsteadily my way.

"Give's a drink," he said.

"What'll it be?"

"Give's a drink." He leaned his head back and surveyed the dancers, raising his eyelids heavily, acting drunker than he was. "I got some wine — me and Nick. It's out in his car... Where's all the fuckin' women? Be with you in a minute, wait here. I'm gonna get a dance."

He set his course across the middle of the hall, picking his way through the crowd until I lost sight of him. I sat down on one of the benches and rolled another smoke and waited. Five minutes later, with no sign of Sully, I took up where I'd left off and made for the exit.

This was October. The night air outside was chilling after the sweaty atmosphere of the dance hall.

Beyond the range of the doorlight I heard voices in the dark, and one of them hollered, "Hey, where you going?"

It was Sully again — transmigrated. He was with Nick Doyle, they were standing at the entrance to the parking lot.

"I'm going home, there's nothing happening around here," I said.

"Hold on, now. I thought you were going to wait for me?"

"I did."

"Stick around for Christsake. We got a bottle in the car — Give him a drink, Nick — Go on with Nick and he'll give you a drink — I'll be right back." Leaving us he trotted up the stone steps and through the door. Nick shrugged. He gestured for me to follow him, leading me past a row of parked cars until we came to his, a cumbersome old Mercury sedan with red bolts of lightning painted along the sides. We climbed into the front seat and for a minute neither of us said anything, listening to the dance hall throbbing and strumming like a monstrous music box. Then Nick let out a squawk like he'd been stung, his voice high-pitched and scratchy.

"Lord Jesus Christ!"

I looked at him.

"We gotta get something to drink. You got any money?" he said.

This Nick Doyle was a few years older than me and I didn't know him too well, he was just another guy I'd seen around — one of Sully's numerous friends. He was thin as a rail and used to be an apprentice harness racing driver before the track closed down.

"Sure. Ten cents."

"Jesus Christ! That's no good."

We continued to sit there, and I looked at him, waiting, and he fidgeted a bit. At length he said, "We got a wine here. You want a drop?"

"I might as well — seeing that I'm here."

Reaching under the dashboard he came up with a quart of Hermit Canadian sherry, the wino's delight, unscrewed the cap and took a generous swallow before passing the bottle to me. I could feel his eyes on me, watching like a hawk, in case I gave the bottle too good a rip. When I handed it back he said, "You know that old quiff at the door?"

"Donovan?"

"The old cocksucker wouldn't let me in for nothing tonight. I ain't paying seventy five cents to get into that jeezless place. There's no tail in there anyway. He wouldn't let me in free, the old quiff." He mused on that for a few seconds. "You know why?"

"I didn't see him letting me in free."

"No, but he never used to charge me. I gave him a good tip on a race once. But he caught me last Saturday smuggling a gallon of wine in. Dearborn bought it and give it to me to take in, I had it under my coat, a whole fucking gallon. Anybody could've seen it, I looked like I was knocked up!"

I felt like saying, "You're as bad as your crazy brother." The Bishop we called him, with his gallons of mass wine, stealing them off the nuns.

"The old cocksucker says to me, 'You're not coming in here with that, Doyle — out you go.' I was drunker'n a jeezly owl. I was gonna put the boots right to him!" He cackled like a hen, pausing to pour down another drink, then sticking the bottle under the dash.

"What do you want, for Jesussake!" Someone was pounding on the window — a weasel-like face peered in at us.

Nick rolled down the window. "What's eating you, Harris?"

"Where's Sully?"

"How in hell should I know?"

"I have to find Sully," he said. He left us and reeled towards the dance hall, hollering at the top of his lungs: "Sully! Sully!"

"He's all drunked-up," said Nick. "That's what I get for showing him the cork." He spit out the window and rolled it up again. "You better go get Sullivan," he said, "and Dearborn — he'll have some money. But leave that leech Harris there."

The dance was raging stronger than ever when I went back in, showing my ticket stub to old Donovan at the door. I jostled through the mob and found Sully leaning against the stage in front of the band. He'd already found Dearborn himself — and Harris had found the two of them. The amplifiers were blasting full force. I shouted in Sully's ear, he nodded, and took Dearborn by the arm and we trooped out with Harris tagging behind — the leech, Nick called him — he was a hard guy to lose —

"Where do you think you're going, Harris?" said Sully.

"That jeezly dance is no good — I'm going with Nick — we're gonna get some more booze—"

"You got any money?"

"No."

"Well, then fuck off."

"I got fifty cents."

"Okay. C'mon."

Dearborn had a dollar – Dearborn Holmes, his name was – He looked like an Oriental, a Chinese manservant – straight out of the movies – eyes half-closed, high cheekbones, an obliging smile glued to his face, shy, never saying a word. He wasn't Chinese but he looked something like it.

We were ten cents short of the price of a bottle.

"And one bottle's no goddamn good, not with five guys," said Nick once we were in the car. "Give us that fifty cents and get out, Harris – you had enough to drink tonight."

"Piss on that."

Nick started the car, and we drove out of the parking lot, and at the first stop sign he turned in his seat and said, "What time is it, Harris?"

Harris squinted in the dark. He was sitting in the back between myself and Dearborn. "A quarter after eleven."

"Let me see that."

"What?"

"That ain't right. Let me see that watch."

Harris poked his wrist forward and Nick caught it and slipped the watch off and examined it. "Hmm." He dropped the watch into his pocket and we sped off. The next street was Water Street and we turned left and tore off upriver in the direction of Clifton.

"Give us me jeezless watch back."

"You don't need a watch, Harris."

"What do you mean? Give us me watch back, Nick."

"Shutup. You want something to drink or don't you?"

"You're not gonna pawn me fuckin' watch, Nick—"

"There's a guy in Clifton that'll give us a good price," Nick said to the rest of us. "Got a nice expansion bracelet on it too."

As we cleared the outskirts of town, racing past the sawmill at Melburn's Cove, it's great cones of sawdust as high as pyramids, Sully said, "I had a dance with the Delaney one – did you see me?"

"I wouldn't mind ridin' that," said Nick.

"A fuckin' pig," said Harris, grumbling, thinking about his watch.

"That's the kind a lad wants," said Nick.

"I give her a little feel," said Sully. "We were waltzing around there and I let the old mitt slide down on her ass, real smooth. She didn't do nothing for a second. Then she says, 'Sully, will you get your finger outa me hole.' Talk about romantic!"

About a mile or so from Clifton we swung around a tight bend and up a rise and bounded onto a straightaway – and then Nick had his foot on the brake – the first time since we left Bannonbridge –

"What is it, Nick?"

"Looks like an accident ahead."

On both sides of the road cars were pulled over, dark figures moving across the headlights. Nick drew off to the shoulder and we came to a stop behind the last car on our side and climbed out. Most of the crowd was knotted around a Volkswagen overturned in the ditch. Elbowing my way up close I got a good view of a man in a long overcoat lying on his back by the open door of the car, one gloved hand resting across his face, as though shading his eyes from a glare — There was a terrific fuss going on around him, everyone asking questions, excited — Nobody knew what had happened. Some of them were hollering instructions — Get an ambulance! — Send for a doctor! — Don't move him! — Get him out of there! — Raise his head! — Unbutton his collar! —

I was in close, heard the injured man mumble something, just audible. "Shh!" Everyone yelled for silence— "He's trying to say something! Shh! Listen!" The man's voice was weak, faint— "What's he saying?" I leaned closer to listen — the people around strained to hear—

"Shutup... I'm the patient..." he said. "I want a nurse..."

Harris was at my elbow — gawking, mouth hanging open— "He wants a nurse!" he shouted, jumping up and down — he disappeared into the crowd, hollering for a nurse, charging around like a maniac —

A young woman knelt beside the man. "I'm a nurse. Just relax, don't move and don't say anything. You'll be all right."

"I want to get out of here." With his hand still shielding his face he tried to raise himself — A half dozen hands shot out and restrained him — everyone shouting at him, "Don't move — stay there—" The injured man subsided with a groan. Then he said to the nurse, "Hold my hand."

The crowd meanwhile continued to swell — every car that came along stopped — it was Saturday night, there was lots of traffic — There was a terrible din, everyone jabbering and shouting at once – they all knew what to do — "Call a doctor!" – "Someone get a flashlight!" – "Let's take him to the hospital!" – "Don't move him!"

An enormous fat man was down on his knees, peering into the upturned car, cupping his eyes against the window – he suddenly looked up –

"There's someone else in the car!"

New excitement – a fresh profusion – "Another one!" The cry was taken up – "Get a flashlight, there's another one!"

Someone stepped forward, the beam of a torch dancing on the car – "Here's a light" – They shone it into the car – it was empty –

The fat man struggled to his feet, looking sheepishly around, mumbling lamely, "I thought... coulda swore I saw..." Nobody was listening – "It sure looked like..." Shrinking into the crowd –

"Was anybody else with you?" asked the nurse. The man on the ground shook his head.

"What's your name?"

"I don't... I can't remember..."

Harris was back again, he'd squeezed himself up close and was kneeling at the man's feet, for some reason gripping him by the ankles – "He doesn't remember!" he exclaimed.

"My name... my name's..."

"Shh! Quiet everyone! He's going to tell his name!"

"Donnie..."

"His name's Donnie!"

"Donnie... Doyle..."

"Holy Jesus!" The words were no sooner out than Harris leapt to his feet. "Stand back, everyone! Stand back — it's Donnie Doyle! His brother's here!"

With his name revealed the man removed the gloved hand from his face — it was sudden — like a magic trick — from a total stranger to someone we know — the Bishop — and the broken bottle beside him, the neck of a gallon jug. I should have known.

Harris went running through the crowd knocking people out of the way, hunting for Nick. "Out of me way, for Christsake! Nick! Where are you? — It's Donnie! Out of me way! It's his brother—"

Nick came round the overturned car and stood gazing down at the Bishop — everyone hushed. He looked abstractedly around, then back at his brother. "By Jesus, so it is."

I thought I'd go find Sully and tell him the news. I crossed the ditch and spied him wandering up the highway from the car, wiping his lips.

"The Bishop? Go on." It was a name Donnie had, left over from when he was an altarboy — he'd been a fanatic altarboy —

"Yeah, it's him all right." I showed him the neck of the gallon jug — I'd picked it up —

"Get rid of that."

"Sure." I tossed it into the trees. Sully was as bad as Harris — he took off like a flash, scrambling across the ditch, pushing his way to the upturned car. "Get a fuckin' doctor — don't move him! His back might be broke — don't touch him, give him air — get an ambulance — loosen his collar — someone get a fuckin' doctor!"

The nurse stiffened, glaring at the intruder. "*Watch* your language."

"Fuck you – he might be dying."

"Don't *swear*!"

"Fuck off." Sully shoved her aside and knelt on one knee by the victim's head. "How do you feel, Bishop? Can you hear me? Can you move your legs? Someone get a doctor!"

Beside me – *sotto voce* – "Did you hear that? He called him Bishop – I thought so – the black coat—"

"He looks young–"

"That guy should watch his tongue – swearing like that in front of a Bishop–"

Nick had recovered himself. He caught hold of me, he wanted to go fetch a doctor. I told him there was one on the way. "We can get one faster," he said.

"Yeah, and we might need one faster – with you driving–"

"What?"

"There's a doctor on his way. Some guy told me he phoned one."

"I'll go myself."

"There he is now." A man carrying a small black bag was being let through the crowd, a path opening for him. Catching sight of him, Harris – the stupid arse – bellowed at the top of his voice, "Is there a doctor in the crowd?"

The doctor stood over the Bishop.

"What's your name?" he said curtly.

"Donnie."

"Donnie who?"

"Donnie Doyle."

"Can you move your arms and legs?"

"Yes..." The Bishop demonstrated by raising each limb a little.

The doctor was a tall good-looking young man, impatience on his face, annoyance — like he'd been called from his girlfriend's bed or something. "Is there an ambulance or car to take him to the hospital?"

"We can take him," said Nick.

Harris: "That's his brother!"

"Okay, put him in the car and take him to the hospital." With that he turned and left.

It was a three-ring circus getting the Bishop into the car — Harris and Sully arguing about the proper way to lift him, Nick cursing them — Dearborn smiling, straining, doing most of the actual lifting —

"Not that way, Harris, you stupid bastard."

"Get his legs, Sully — get a good holt on him—"

"I know what I'm doing — I know how to carry a wounded man."

"Lift, you cocksuckers!"

"Watch it now — he's falling—"

"Let me show yez — Harris, smarten up — I know how to do this the right way—"

"You don't know fuck-all."

They staggered up the side of the ditch, one of the Bishop's legs dragging over the ground. I stood back and watched them. The way they were jumping around you couldn't get near to help. "Hold his head up — " "All together — " "Easy now — " "Wait'll I get a better grip—"

Against all odds they maneuvered him into the back seat, Sully and Harris and Dearborn underneath him, supporting him on their laps. I got into the front seat with Nick. We were already pointed towards

Clifton, which was less than a mile away, but instead of driving to the hospital there Nick turned into the first yard and backed out to go in the other direction.

"What're you doing, Nick?" said Sully. "Take him to Clifton – it's shorter."

Nick scowled – his teeth clenched tight – he shifted the gears angrily. "The hell with you. We're going to Bannonbridge."

"That was Doctor Fliegher – he's from Clifton – he'll be looking for us there."

"The hell with that doctor, he's no good. You saw him – he didn't give a fuck." We were just under way when a cop appeared on the road – stepping out of his car, the red light on the roof flashing – he flagged us down – he'd just arrived on the scene –

"That's him, is it?" He shone his flashlight on the Bishop groaning in the back.

"Where'll we take him?" said Harris.

The cop paused, looking down the road. "Bannonbridge, I guess – since that's the way you're headed."

We roared off, Nick with the gas pedal to the floor. In no time at all we were doing ninety-five miles an hour, careening around turns, catching and passing everything on the road. It didn't bother the drunks in the back seat – I could hear them – trying to cheer the Bishop up. "You're okay, kid, nothing to worry about – just take it easy and we'll soon have you there – " "We'll get you to the hospital, you'll be all right, as good as new – " "You'll have a great time with all those nurses – " "That'll be the life – a nice soft bed – riding the nurses – " "Jeez, I wouldn't mind going to the hospital myself – " A pause. "Where'd you get the car, anyway?" The Bishop moaned. "I don't know..."

"You don't know?"

"I... I..."

"What?"

"I stole it."

"Jesus!" Nick squawked like a scalded chicken. "I knew it! You son of a whore. Where'd you get it?"

"At the dance... the keys were in it... so I took it."

Harris suddenly noticed how fast we were going. "Slow 'er down some, Nick." We were flying – the road to Bannonbridge nothing but hills and turns, the car straining to hold the road –

"Fuck you. I should run 'er up the bank. That rotten bastard..." He snarled, talking to himself. "Nothing but trouble since the day he was born... lousy bastard... if he'd get himself killed it'd be all right..."

"C'mon now, Nick," said Harris. "The Bishop's a good lad–"

"Jesus, shutup! And don't call him that."

"It's only because he got hit on the head by a puck that time–"

"Shutup, you cocksucker – I'll strangle you–"

Harris lowered his voice. "You're okay, Bishop, you'll be down with them nurses in no time." "

They were quiet for a moment – a tense serious business, this – racing to the hospital with an accident victim – then Sully said, "Listen, Bishop, have you got a hard-on?"

Dearborn snorted – the first peep out of him all night –

"Come off it, Sully," said Harris. "Have some sense."

"It's not funny," groaned the Bishop. The accident must have shook him up good – he hadn't said a thing in Latin – he'd forgotten his liturgy altogether.

"I'm serious. If you got a hard-on that means your back is broken. Have you got one?"

"No."

"There, now. Nothing to worry about."

We shot into town like a bolt of lightning – streaking along Water Street – through two stop signs, swinging up the Hospital Hill with screeching tires. Nick turned his head to the backseat, said fiercely, "Now I'll handle this so keep your goddamn traps shut – I don't want to hear a word – " He returned his eyes to the road, the row of dark elms up the hill racing by – "You rotten cocksuckers – "

With the hospital upon us on our left Harris said, "In here, Nick, go in here –"

"Harris, you prick – you *prick* – I said shut your fuckin' mouth, you rotten cocksucker – " He was beside himself, raging – fit to kill – "You think I don't know where we are – "

"We just want to help," said Sully.

"And you too –"

We came to a jolting halt beneath the light of the Emergency Entrance and everyone got out, leaving the Bishop sprawled on the back seat. Harris ran up to the doorbell, to get there first. When he raised his hand to ring it he yelped; he'd been holding the Bishop's head and his hand was wet with blood. He held both hands before his eyes – they were both bloody. He shoved them in Nick's face. "God, Nick, look at this —"

"Shutup, Harris."

Pushing him out of the way Nick pressed the bell button. He kept his finger on the bell for a good minute, then gave a dozen or so short rings. We could hear it clanging loudly in the halls beyond the door but nobody came. We all peered through the glass door.

"I'll go try the front," said Harris. He set off at a run and disappeared around the corner of the building.

"I'll go with him," said Sully.

"You stay here. There they are now." Seeing two nurses coming towards us he took his finger off the button. One of the double doors opened slightly – the nurses looked out at us – unable to conceive what we'd be doing there – like we had the wrong address. One of them said, "What do you want? Why are you ringing the bell." Her voice was icy.

"We got an accident victim," said Nick.

The nurses exchanged glances. Then the one who'd spoke said, "Is there a doctor here for him?"

"How should we know?"

"The doctor at the accident was from Clifton," said Sully.

"Oh? Well, he won't come down here. You should have gone to Clifton."

"Yeah, well we didn't," said Nick.

"The cops told us to come to Bannonbridge," said Sully.

The nurses looked at each other again – they didn't want to be bothered with all this –

"You'll have to go to Clifton. We can't take him here."

"Like hell you can't. He's hurt – C'mon, get a move on."

"The guy's dying," said Sully

They didn't give up easily – they tried to send us away, but we wouldn't budge. Finally one of them shrugged. "Okay, then. Just a minute. But you shouldn't have come here..." They left the door and walked back along the hall and around a turn.

"Let's get him in there," said Sully.

"Wait'll they come back. They must've gone for a stretcher."

"Fuck the stretcher. We can carry him. We don't want to lose no time–"

The Bishop wasn't thin like Nick – just the opposite – he weighed a good two hundred pounds. "Get around the other side, Dearborn, take his head. We'll ease him out. You got to be careful, he might have a broken back–"

We were lugging him through the door, in a fashion, when the nurses arrived with a high trundle bed – and not a moment too soon. Dearborn had the Bishop by the middle, cradling him like a rolled carpet, his legs buckling – grunting, face flushed, making staggering little steps – Nick holding his brother's feet – Sully darting back and forth like a ferret, giving instructions. I had a partial grip on the other side of the Bishop's middle, facing Dearborn, but I had to let go and step aside so he could be placed on the bed. Dearborn's eyes popped from the strain – his smile gone –

"Lift him on, Dearborn – hoist him–"

"I can't..."

"Don't drop him, for Christsake!"

There was a helpless look on Dearborn's face, he was weakening, the body sinking – "I can't–"

"Oh!" The nurses didn't know what to do. They could see it coming, a crash-landing. The Bishop knew it too, and suddenly he came to life; it was either that or take a nose-dive to the floor; he caught hold of the bed and pulled himself onto it, then lay back moaning and groaning. Dearborn's Chinese smile seeped back. We wheeled the Bishop down the hall and stopped at an elevator door and a nurse pressed the button. While we were waiting Harris materialized from a stairwell at one end of the hall and called out, "Is he okay? How is he?" He ran up to us, breathless, and informed the nurses at the top of his voice that Nick was the accident victim's brother.

"Will you please not talk so loud." The nurse shook her arm out of his grasp. "There are patients in this hospital trying to sleep."

We crowded into the elevator, and as it began its lumbering ascent from the basement Sully stared at Harris's hands, appearing to notice them for the first time. The drama was too great for him, his sense of proportion abandoned him – "Harris, your hands are covered with blood! Are you hurt? Good God, what happened?" The concern, the pathos – from Sully! – who couldn't care less if Harris had both arms chopped off at the elbows – it was television, from watching Dr. Kildare. Harris hesitated to answer, the possibility hadn't occurred to him, that he'd been injured in the line of duty. He looked hedgingly at his hands, wondering if they could really be cut – pulling the

Bishop from the smoking wreckage – if he could get away with it –

"You stupid bastard, it's Donnie's blood – you know that," spat out Nick.

"How in fuck was I to know?" said Sully – he gave Nick a sullen look –

"That'll be enough of that kind of language." The nurses were both aloof, inhospitable. We reached the third floor and wheeled the patient down the terrazzo tiles, through the smell of the hospital, like an invisible fog of disinfectants, medicines, laundry, sickness, sterilization. We turned in at an empty double room and transferred the Bishop onto one of the beds. He edged himself over from the trundle, not trusting our methods. Where his head had been resting there was a pool of blood. He lay on his back now, with his eyes shut, moaning steadily.

"Are you comfortable, Bishop?" said Harris.

"I don't feel so good." His voice was feeble.

"Who's his doctor?" said the nurse, the one who seemed to be in charge.

Pale as a ghost the Bishop raised himself up on one arm. "I think I'm going to throw up." The words were followed by an enormous gush of vomit. We jumped back, scattering out of the line of fire – but it was too late for the nurse, she was directly in front of the Bishop and caught the flood full on, all down the front of her uniform. The Bishop lay back again, panting. The nurse stood with her arms outstretched – like wings – surveying herself, looking her uniform up and down – then she fled the room. I was right behind her, hand to my mouth. The smell was overpowering. It took a minute before my stomach subsided — I had to put my mind on something else — Dearborn was out in the hall too — prowling around looking in doorways —

"Where were you?" I asked him.

"I came up the stairs. The elevator was too full. Where'd they put him?"

I indicated the room I'd left.

"How is he?"

"I don't know. He just puked."

"Yeah. I thought so, I saw the nurse going by. She's washing in a room back there."

"It's that wine — God — the stink of it—"

Dearborn had a better stomach than I did. He strolled into the Bishop's room and didn't come charging out again.

In a few minutes the nurse came back, cleaned up now, a new apron on. She eyed me questioningly. I told her I was waiting for the others. "Well, you can't wait out here," she said. She showed me the visitors' lounge. I went in and sat down. The floor was carpeted — there were a couple of floor lamps, a couch, several easy chairs, magazines on a coffee table, nondescript prints on the wall. I rolled a smoke and thumbed through a copy of Life magazine. Before long Sully came in and flopped on the couch.

"Nothing the matter with him," he said. Sully the consultant physician.

"You must have sinus trouble," I said. "That poor nurse—"

He didn't hear me. He was in a reverie. "You have to know how to carry a man, in case his back's broken." There was an expression of sublime self-satisfaction on his face." I don't know *too* much about it – Oh no, not *too* much."

"But his back wasn't broken, we knew that," I said. "He could move his legs."

"That don't matter. It might've been broken."

"But it wasn't."

"But it *might've* been."

"But we knew it wasn't."

"Yes, but it *might've* been."

"Forget it."

"No, but it *might've* been broken. You have to know the right way to carry a guy, in an accident like that–"

At that moment a priest wandered into the room. He was quite old and balding, the few hairs on his scalp a light silver, and he walked with a nervous shake – jerking along like a mechanical toy. I knew him slightly, who he was, Father Noonan, had seen him around. He spoke with a rapid mumble, the words rolling around in his mouth and dropping out like marbles.

"Poor Donnie, poor Donnie," he said.

"How is he, Father?" said Sully.

"Oh, he's okay, I think. He's not too badly hurt." He sat down and took out a cigarette and lit it.

"Give us your makin's," Sully said. I tossed him the tobacco and papers.

"He stole the car, did he?" said the priest.

"I guess so," I said.

Sully gave me a sharp look. "We don't know, Father, we just found him there. We don't know nothing about it."

We sat for a moment in silence, the three of us smoking. Then Harris came in the door, his hands still bloodstained, and sank into the chair. He sighed wearily.

"Roll me a smoke, will you," he said to me, holding his hands up by way of explanation. He sighed again.

"He was drinking, I suppose," said the priest, when Harris had his cigarette going.

Harris nodded – ponderously – sighing – "Yes, Father, I believe he was."

"A bad thing, a bad thing," said the priest. "Does no one any good, drinking. It causes nothing but trouble."

Another silence ensued. It was broken by Sully.

"We might as well admit it, Father," he said. "We're drinking tonight too." He was sitting at an angle from the priest – I caught him wink –

Father Noonan nodded. "I know, I know."

This out of Harris. "I wish I could stop."

The priest sat up and stared at him. "Stop? What do you mean, you wish you could stop? You're just a kid yet. How long have you been drinking, five years?"

"Well... yeah, about that, Father."

Sully scoffed. "Come out of that, Harris, you haven't been drinking more than a year."

"Yes, I have, I been drinking longer than that. I started about three years ago."

"My arse," said Sully.

"Three years?" said the priest. "You could stop anytime. You don't know what it is to be enslaved by liquor."

"Well I do," said Sully emphatically. "I can't stop – I know, I've tried."

"How long have you been drinking?"

"About six years."

"Do you want to quit? That's the thing. Do you want to quit?"

"Do I? There's nothing I want more in the world." I looked at Sully – I had to shake my head in amazement–

The priest slowly stretched his legs out. "Well then, why don't you?"

"I've tried, for Christsake. I've tried but it don't work. I was going to quit gradually, cut down a bit at a time – but it was no good. I found out I can't do it that way. What I'm like, if I take one drink I'm gone for the night. It's got to be all or nothing for me."

The priest nodded knowingly. "I understand – I know just what it's like. Let me tell you boys something." He leaned forward confidentially, lowering his voice. "I don't want you to be shocked. But – " pause – "I'm an alcoholic myself." He settled back in his chair to receive the reaction.

"Yeah, I know," said Sully.

The priest glanced at him quickly. "Yes, an alcoholic. Not many people know that – that is – " He looked at Sully again, frowning a moment – "but I haven't had a drink in years. I can't take a drink – People think because I'm a priest, that it couldn't happen, but it doesn't matter – it can happen to anyone. I can't take even a single drop. If I have one drink, that's it, I'm finished, I can't stop until I see the bottom of the bottle – and after that it's another bottle – and another–"

Sully shook his head — as though astonished at the coincidence, how similar it was to himself — with a different laugh — his weakness out in the open — sharing his dark secret with another tormented soul. "That's exactly the way it is with me, Father."

"Me too," said Harris.

"Go 'way, Harris, for Jesus sake." Sully turned on him contemptuously. "You don't know what it's like to be drunk."

"Well I know," said the priest — "and not only from my own experiences. I've been with more winos in my time than you boys will ever lay eyes on, all of you together. I know what it's like — And let me tell you, they lead pitiful lives — they aren't to be envied, I can assure you — *pitiful* lives."

"But how can I quit?" said Sully. "What's the way out? I'd like someone to tell me that."

"Yeah," said Harris.

"If you're really serious you should go down to the AA's. There you'll hear some really hardened veterans talk. They'll tell you what it's like. If anyone knows how to quit they do."

Sully gave this his consideration.

"I couldn't go down there," he said. "They'd think I was just a punk kid."

"No they won't, no they won't."

"I don't know..."

"All right, don't go. Don't go down there. Go out and get another quart of wine and get drunk again. Live your life that way."

"No, but I want to stop." Sully's voice became very quiet... solemn... the room was still. "It's killing my mother. I don't care about the old man, he can die tomorrow — but the old lady..."

"The same with me," said Harris. "If she knew—"

I squirmed in my chair. Sully was outdoing himself. I was on the brink of getting up and leaving when a doctor appeared in the doorway and said brusquely, "Get out of here and go home. You're making too much noise."

We all looked at each other — at the severe tone of his voice — We got to out feet, except for the priest—

"Where did the car come from?" said the doctor. He was middleaged, in a peppergray suit and vest.

"Nobody knows," said Sully. "We just found him in the ditch lying beside it."

The doctor studied us. "Weren't you with him?"

"No, we were driving to Clifton when we saw the car in the ditch."

"Oh, I'm sorry." His expression eased somewhat. "I thought you were with him."

"No, we found him by the road," said Sully. "We were just driving along. What do you think the cops will do?"

"I don't know."

"Is he hurt bad?"

"Nothing serious. A slight concussion."

The doctor turned and left. Since we were standing we decided we might as well leave too — go out to the car and wait for Nick and Dearborn — there was no more help we could offer —

We took the stairs down, and on the ground floor Sully said, "You'd better wash your hands, Harris. You can't go downtown like that. There's a washroom over there."

"Yeah..." Harris was reluctant to erase the evidence of his heroism of the night – but Sully insisted – "You can't walk around like that, you look like you been fingering a broad with the rag on."

"Okay." Taking a deep breath – another sigh – "I better get this blood off."

"We'll be outside. Don't take too long."

Once out the door Sully grabbed my arm and said, "Let's go, before he comes."

"Where?"

"I just remembered that bottle in the car. There's still half a quart left. We better get it and take off."

"What about Nick – and Dearborn?"

We ran along the row of darkened basement windows towards the Emergency Entrance.

"Never mind them. They won't want any. You heard what the priest said, it's bad stuff. It'd just ruin their lives."

§

The Black Horse was the only tavern in town, so you were shit out of luck if you got barred from it; and they must have barred Ralph Ramsay a dozen times.

"This is it, Ralph, out you go! And this time it's final, don't come back again" – MacPherson the waiter hustling Ralph to the door – slamming it behind him – and Ralph staggering off in the night –

A couple of days later I asked MacPherson what Ralph had been guilty of this last time.

"He stood right up on one of the tables," MacPherson said, "ranting at everybody. 'You're all a bunch of arseholes!' he says, 'a bunch of nobodies, you're nothing!' You know the way he goes on. 'What's any of you guys ever done?' he says. 'Tell me that? What kind of mark are you guys gonna leave behind when you're dead? You're all full of shit' – You know what he gets like. The man's crazy, he should be put away."

Other times Ralph had been barred for bumming money around the tables, or playing his trumpet, or breaking glasses, or starting fights, or any combination of these things. Sully had been barred with him a few times, but Sully was not so unpredictable, he was less given to explosive outbursts. By himself it°s unlikely he'd have been barred more than a few times.

A couple of weeks later, in the normal course of events, the two of them would drift in the door and sit quietly in the corner. "Okay if we have a drink, MacPherson? We just dropped in for a quick one."

MacPherson was by nature a kind and easygoing man, and by this time would have forgiven or forgotten about the last incident, and he'd serve them like any other customers in good standing.

Ralph got wild like this only when he was drunk, and even then only sometimes, when the mood struck him. Normally he was a sensitive and thoughtful person. He was about thirty years old – or thirty-five

— or maybe forty; it was hard to say. He'd been around as long as I could remember, always looking the same, with his beard and his thick hair hanging over his collar. He was considered an eccentric by the locals, I guess with some justification.

One day, in fact it was the afternoon of Christmas day, Ralph dropped around to my old man's place while I was washing the dishes. It was freezing cold outside but he had no coat on. He looked haggard. He sat down at the kitchen table and told me he hadn't slept all night. "I can't sleep anymore," he said. "I never could. I don't know what's wrong with me. I walk around all night and then when daylight comes I go home and go to bed. When everyone else is getting up I'm turning in. Every night it's the same. The cops are starting to look at me. One of these days they're going to arrest me."

"What for?"

"I don't know. For impersonating a human being." He had a laugh at that.

Because it was Christmas there was a quart of rye sitting on the counter. After eyeing it for a few minutes Ralph said, "You mind if I have a taste of that?"

"Here." I poured him a drink.

"That's nice stuff. Very smooth. Did you get that for Christmas?"

"Yeah, from myself."

"I got some liquor too. I mean my mother did. No, I guess it was me. I was at home last night and there were gifts under the tree, and I thought, this must be mine, *Evening in Paris,* so I drank it. Yeah, I got lots of booze. It's all gone now, I drank it last night. The old lady doesn't know yet. *Chanel No. 5,* that's another one. One of these days I'll go into some posh bar, I'll be standing there looking sophisticated, and the bartender'll say, 'What's yours, sir? What are you going to have?' 'Oh, I guess I'll have an *Evening in Paris*. On the rocks.' It's so long since I had the real stuff I forget what it's called. Shaving lotion, vanilla extract, rubbing alcohol—perfume! As long as it comes in a bottle that's the important thing. You can't drink the labels."

He'd brought his trumpet with him, which was about the only thing he owned, apart from his clothes. "I want to play you a number," he said, "something in season." He put the trumpet to his lips and played *O Holy Night* – In a small room like our kitchen it almost blew the roof off. He was a good musician at times, when it suited him. He'd been playing the trumpet for years and years, ever since he was a boy. Several times he attempted to play with local dance bands but it never worked out. He couldn't read music and he had his own ideas about arrangements, and he had difficulty keeping sober. He claimed the other musicians were unimaginative and mediocre, which they probably were. He was, you might say, an artist who relied on inspiration, and his temperament made it difficult to adjust to other musicians and regular dates. So now he played for himself and his friends and once a year entered the Sanatarium Fund amateur night where he was always a big hit but never won a prize.

"Thank you, Ralph, that was very nice," I said.

"I lost my teeth last night," he said. "I had all my teeth pulled a few months ago and got a plate, but

I left my coat somewhere and my teeth were in the pocket. Dr. Reid pulled all my teeth out – Look." He opened his mouth, revealing the bare gums. "He said he was going to give me a plate – I told him, why not throw in a cup and saucer while you're at it, a plate's no good by itself. This is great stuff. You don't mind if I have another one?" I poured him another rye. I remember Ralph saying once he'd gone to a doctor because he thought he had ulcers, and the doctor wanted to know about his drinking habits. "He gave me this test, it was a list of twenty questions to find out if someone's an alcoholic, and if you answered yes to four of them that meant you were. There were things like, Do you drink because you feel shy with people, Do you crave a drink in the morning, Do you drink to escape worries or troubles – there were twenty of them, and I answered yes to them all – except one. And that was, Does your drinking interfere with your work? I put down no for that one." Ralph hadn't worked a week in his life.

He took a pull on his glass of rye, then sat there a moment silently. When he spoke his voice sounded suddenly sad. "No work, no money, no women, nothing," He said. "I've got the feeling I'm just watching life go by and I can't do a thing about it." He shook his head. "I came here to play a song and have a few drinks and be happy, but it's no good. You know, everybody around this town thinks I'm a bum. Everybody does. I can't get a girl, not a chance. You want to know something that happened? I asked a girl out a couple of weeks ago. I said, how'd you like to go out with me some night, we could go to a show or something. Do you know what she answered? I wouldn't go to the shithouse with you. How would you like it if a girl said that to you? That's pretty bad, eh? A girl has no right to say that to a man, no matter who she is or what she thinks of you. But that's my status around here. Just because I don't have a job and live like everyone else... I'm an individual – I don't have to do what everyone wants me to do. I may not have much in this life but I've got my own mind. What I should do is get out of this town. I should, but I don't. Why don't I just get out? Tell me that?"

"I don't know. It's up to you."

"I guess so." He was quiet again. Then he said, "Well, I'll have to go home and see my mother and father. Then it's back to my own estate on Water Street. My parents, they watch me like two cats to see I don't step out of line. But I'm always drunk just the same. I've got nothing else to do. I'm an alcoholic. I can prove it, just ask me twenty questions. I drink and I don't do anything else."

"How much do you drink anyway, Ralph?"

"How much? As much as I can get. I'd be drinking twenty-four hours a day if I could afford it. But I've got no money. I'm living on welfare. Did you know that? Me, on welfare. What do you think of that? I get sixty dollars a month. I give my mother and father forty and keep the rest. So I have to go bumming on the streets to get enough for a drink. That's how low I've come. I bum money down on the front street. A bum." He got to his feet, still holding his glass with an inch of rye in it. "I have to try and find my coat. My scarf is in the pocket, and my teeth. But I don't care about the teeth. I hardly ever wear them anyway."

"They must make eating easier."

"No, I don't eat with them. They aren't comfortable. They're just decorations. I only wear them at special times, like when someone asks me out." He laughed. "Yeah, when I'm asked out, that's the only time I wear them. Anyway, I've got to get going. What time is it now? I'm going blind, I can't even see that clock there."

"It's twenty-to-five."

"There, I'm late already." He emptied his glass and at the door shouted over his shoulder, "Merry Christmas and a Happy New Year!"

There was one detail about Ralph's visit that I didn't pay attention to. Shortly before leaving he went to the bathroom. When he came out he didn't stay around much longer. I learned why the following afternoon.

Ralph was at the door and came sheepishly in. "The thief returns to the scene of the crime," he said.

"Yeah?" I didn't know what he meant.

"Ah me. I'm cold sober. I woke up this morning ready to put down a big drink of rum, I had it hid away under the bed, and I was thinking by God it's good to have a drink in the morning, I need one real bad, and I've got a pint of rum sitting there under the bed. A pint of rum!" And he started laughing to himself. "Yes, that's the way to start the day. I had it all figured out. I didn't touch the pint last night, saving it for the morning so I could start the day off right. Well, that's what you get. Crime doesn't pay! The thief returns to the scene of the crime."

"What are you talking about, Ralph?"

"Have you got a beer? You wouldn't have a beer in the house?"

It being the season the fridge was stocked, so I got out a couple of pints of Schooner.

"Ah, that feels good, nice and cold. Yes sir, I unscrewed the cap and was set to bolt down a big drink the first thing in the morning. By Jesus it's a good thing I didn't. Turpentine! That's the way to start the day – with a good shot of turpentine. Here I thought I had a nice pint of rum and it was turpentine."

Now I understood. Our bathroom was quite a mess at the time, with just myself and the old man living in the apartment, and among other things lying around was a bottle of turpentine for cleaning paint brushes. If you didn't know what it was you'd think it was booze, because the stuff was in a rum bottle. Ralph had spotted it when he went to take a leak and thought it was the real thing.

°°You mean – you stole that bottle of—"

"That's right. Ah, what a person I am, I°ve got no scruples, I come here and drink your liquor and then try to steal more of it. I must have no shame, no conscience at all. I hated to do it. But I saw that pint there and I thought this is just what I need for the morning. Perfume in the evening and the real stuff in the morning. I got up and reached for the bottle this morning with my hands trembling and I took the cap off and started to take a drink. That's what I get. Turpentine! It's punishment for my sins."

Well, we had a bit of a laugh at that and drank a lot of beer. At some stage in the afternoon Ralph once again bemoaned the fact that he was reduced to nothing but a bum and an alcoholic. "I went to the AA's for a while," he said, "I tried to kick the habit. But that's no good. They can't help me. I remember one meeting, you know the way these things go, this guy got up on the platform telling us his life story, what hell his life was when he was drinking and why he had to stop. I don't even know his name, he was some guy from upriver, I never saw him before. This was the first night that Jackie Craig – he'd never been to a meeting before and somebody had talked him into going and he was standing at the back of the room – you could tell he wasn't happy about being there by the look on his face – and this guy up front was saying when he drank he used to beat up his wife and children, really kick them around, little kids and all – he was giving a big description of the terrible things he used to do, and he was going on and on about it, when there was this disgusted voice from the back of the room: 'You rotten bastard. You're not an alcoholic – you're nuts!' It was Jackie. Soon as he said that he turned and walked out."

This particular Christmas coincided with another of Ralph's banishments from the tavern, for what reason I don't remember. Being barred wasn't all that much an inconvenience, there were plenty of places to drink provided you could come up with the price of a bottle. Ralph's old room, for example, in the old Kelly rooming house by the Station Wharf – a place he despised – or on one of the wharves, or in a boxcar at the CN station, or behind the stores on Water Street where the ground was covered with broken wine and rum bottles. But in the cold weather it was better to be indoors, and in the Black Horse there was always someone there and Ralph enjoyed company.

Much of the time his company was Sullivan, when Sully wasn't running around with myself or Nick or some other ne'er-do-well friend. Sully, I should mention, was twenty years old. He'd retired from school at the age of sixteen, after a couple of years of indifferently trying to get out of the eighth grade, and in the period since he hadn't exactly killed himself working. A day in his life can be described simply enough.

He lived with his parents, and around noon he would get out of bed and have a couple of strips of raw bacon and a bottle of coke for breakfast, then head down to the pool room. He'd spend the afternoon shooting pool or playing the pinball machines or watching others do these two things. If someone came up with a bottle of something he probably wouldn't go home for supper. If not he would go home and eat, not saying a word to his mother and father. They had stopped saying words to him as well, after years of talking at deaf ears. The only exception was once every two or three months when there would be a row over his not getting a job. This accomplished nothing and another several months of silence followed. His father had got him work once as a house painter but Sully lasted only to his first pay cheque, which he blew in two nights of drunken generosity towards his friends. This brought him to the realization that working didn't pay — not two weeks of backbreaking labor for a two night drunk — so he failed to return to the job on Monday, or ever after.

After supper it was down town again where he quite often bumped into Ralph on the street. If there was any money they pooled it and caught the liquor store before it closed. If there was none or not enough they spent the next few hours bumming, or they hunted around to find someone who would buy a bottle for the pleasure of their company, usually some teenager just starting to drink. Then they made for one of the many bootleggers in town.

When the night ended Sully went home to bed. Every day it was more or less the same story.

Sullivan was Ralph's close associate for a number of reasons: they both had the same amount of time on their hands; they had something of an attraction for the bottle; they were misfits and were well aware of it; they weren't stupid people, despite their limited education, and could talk to each other; and they shared an abiding dislike for the town and most of the people in it.

§

Here's a picture of the two of them, taken from the year before Sully and I went to Toronto, when it appeared Sully might never get out of Bannonbridge, not even for the brief time we were away.

A November night, cold, rainy, the kind of rain that hits your skin like frozen needles. Ralph's room is on the second floor at the back corner of his rooming house, it has two windows, one facing the river and the other looking down onto a lane leading up to Water Street. There's a streetlight at the corner of the lane and at intervals sheets of rain gust past the light.

Ralph is standing looking out the window, hands behind his back. Behind him lying on the bed with both shoes planted squarely on the blankets is Sully.

"Well, what are we gonna do?" Sully says, for about the half-dozenth time.

"I don't know, we can't go out in this. Why don't you go to the tavern."

"Screw that. If they won't let you in, the hell with them. They're not gonna get my business. Besides all I got is a quarter. We could go up to the Castle." The Castle is a restaurant in Bannonbridge, a teenage hangout where they do much of their panhandling.

"Won't be anyone there tonight. You'd have to be crazy to be out on a night like this. It wouldn't be worth the walk."

When they're silent you can hear the rain, and from a room above a record player is playing *I Walked in the Garden with Jesus*. When it reaches the end whoever is up there starts it over again. The same hymn has been repeating itself now for over half an hour.

"You know, that could drive you batty," says Sully, staring up at the ceiling. "Who lives up there anyway?"

"I don't know, I don't know anybody in this place. They're all old people. I'm the only one here under seventy. I don't know where they all come from. I see them creeping up and down the stairs and along the halls. They just look at you but they never say anything."

Sully fishes a package of tobacco from his coat pocket and rolls a cigarette, the shredded end flaming briefly when he lights it. "Be great to have a drink now," he says.

"I'm glad you came down," says Ralph, still staring out the window. He shakes his head. "What a goddamn dismal depressing sight. I can't stand being alone in this room anymore, I'd rather be in jail. At least I'd know why I was there. I'm serving a sentence and I haven't been arrested yet. Solitary confinement. It's nice to get a visitor."

"I don't blame you. I couldn't take this place very long myself."

Ralph's room, it's true, doesn't have much to recommend it. It's like a large box papered with brownish wallpaper with yellow stains seeping down from the ceiling. The ceiling itself is a network of cracks and places where the plaster has fallen revealing wooden slats. The furniture consists of a bed, a wooden chair, a small chest of drawers and a table which is now covered with dirty dishes and utensils. The lightbulb is weak, giving the place a dusky atmosphere. There is no heat and the two of them have their coats on.

"Well, what'll we do?" says Ralph.

"Play something, why don't you? Anything to drown out that noise upstairs."

Ralph takes his trumpet out of its dog-eared leather case. Different times he was on the verge of selling it, feeling there was no important reason for keeping it, he wasn't going anywhere, but each time he hadn't been able to go through with it. He knew that once gone it was unlikely he'd ever get the money together to buy it back or get another one.

"What do you want?"

"Play *Ruby*."

Ralph blows on the trumpet but his heart isn't in it. He stops after a short while. "I don't feel like it. I'll play it later."

"That was good, that sounded real good. I wish to hell I could play a trumpet like that, or anything, even a mouth organ."

"Well, you're not too bad a singer. That's enough."

"Yeah, I can sing, I'm a good singer. Maybe we should form a group, just the two of us. We might go places."

Ralph paces the short distance across the room and back.

"It's going to be another cold winter. You know they don't have any heat in this building? If you want heat you have to buy your own heater. Last winter — it was like a refrigerator in here last winter. I can't afford a heater. There should be a law against this, it's no way for a man to live. It might be all right for an Eskimo. But I'm not an Eskimo."

"You can already see your breath."

"And look at these, storm windows they call them, they're supposed to keep out the cold. French safes, they nail big French safes across the windows and leave them on all year and you're protected from the cold." There are plastic coverings over the windows, they had stretched and sagged and they flapped in the wind and distorted the view outside.

"You can't take your clothes off in the winter, I went months and I couldn't take my clothes off for fear of dying of exposure. I wasn't warm one minute for more than six months. That's a hell of a way to live.

I don't want another winter in this hole. I'd rather live in an igloo. What I should do is make myself an igloo this winter and live in that. Even an Eskimo wouldn't live under these conditions."

"At least it's a place to have a drink, it's a good thing they don't bother you that way."

"They don't care. All they care about is your rent."

They hear the sound of slow feet shuffling in the hall, passing the door and ascending the stairs. They listen until the footsteps are gone.

"Another old man," mutters Ralph. "This house is full of old men, they all come here to die. I shouldn't be here. I'm not an old man. I don't belong here."

He picks up his trumpet and blows a deafening defiant blast. A sharp knock sounds on the wall.

"Who's that?" says Sully.

"Another old man. Or maybe it's an old woman. They don't like to hear me playing at night — or anytime for that matter. They want to die quietly."

"What we need — we ought to get out of here, that's what," says Sully. "I mean out of town. We're wasting our talents here, especially you, not so much me since I don't have too many, but I'm getting sick of this place. I'll never get anywhere in a dump like this. We should just get up and get the hell out, just like that. No wasting time."

"Where would we go?"

"Anywhere. Montreal. No, Toronto's better, Montreal's full of crazy Frenchman, we'd never get anywhere there. Toronto."

"You can't go anywhere without money, Sully. How would we get there? What would we live on?"

"It wouldn't take much. I could probably steal enough off the old man to get us started. We take a train up and then we find a job. We could live good up there. The wine's cheaper and there's lots of loose women hanging around. It'd be no problem."

"I don't know anything about Toronto, Sully. They'd never give me a job, a guy my age."

"You play the trumpet, eh? There are hundreds of bands in Toronto, they're always looking for talent. Look, Ralph, for Christsake, you can't wait forever. I mean, around here they don't know a trumpet from a shoe horn – you're crazy hanging around Bannon-bridge."

"I know, I know." Ralph ponders a moment. "You're right, I have to get out of here, that's the only solution. I can't just sit around this town and die." A moment later he says, "Ah, it's no use. We'd never make it . You need money, you need connections, we'd be lost in Toronto."

"C'mon, don't talk like that. I thought you wanted to leave."

"Sure. Sure I want to leave."

Sully gets up off the bed and with a long snorting snuffle inhales his nose clean and spits into the grocery bag Ralph uses for garbage. "Well, make up your mind. I'm ready to go."

"I don't think you are, Sully. If I said, okay, let's pack, you'd make up some excuse for putting it off."

"No I wouldn't." He settles himself back on the bed.

"You know, the worst thing is that they don't give you a chance," says Ralph. The wind and rain are shaking the plastic storm windows, snapping them against the inside windows. "They're only interested in themselves. Well, I don't give a shit about them. Who are they anyway? They're a bunch of nobodies."

"The hell with everybody," says Sully.

"All they want to do is push you into the dirt, they aren't satisfied unless you're crawling in front of them."

"It's no good talking about it. My Christ, I wish we had something to drink, I'm croaking. I should've asked the old man for a few bucks." He adjusts the pillow under his head. "But I wouldn't give the bastard the satisfaction."

"It's not that I'm not good enough. It's not that."

"You're *too* good for them. They can't stand that."

"I just don't get a chance. I'm getting old, I'm an old man now."

"C'mon, Ralph, you're not old. You're a young man. You got a lot of time left and you got the talent. What've I got?"

"Pass me your tobacco."

Ralph rolls a cigarette and lights a match with his thumbnail. He drags on the cigarette and fingers his beard. "I think I'll shave this off," he says.

"What?"

"The beard. I'm going to shave it tomorrow."

"How come? It looks good. Don't be crazy."

"I don't care. I need a change. Maybe I'll try and get a job. That'd be a change, I mean if I can get a job."

"Maybe I should get one too."

"But who'll hire us? They think we're bums."

"The hell with them."

"No, it's no good. Maybe if I shave nobody will know me. They might hire me that way. I could say I'm a stranger in town. What do you think?"

"The hell with them. The best thing to do is to get up to Toronto. There's no future hanging around here. I could be your manager."

"Yeah, my manager. That's what I need, a manager. Okay, you're hired."

"How much of a cut do I get?"

"I'll give you fifty per cent. How's that sound? Fifty per cent of nothing."

"No, I'm serious."

"Okay, I'll pay you in advance. How about..." He reaches in his pocket and pulls out a ball of paper which he opens. It's a two dollar bill. "How about fifty per cent of a bottle of wine?"

"Hey! Where'd you get that? Here we've been sitting around here—"

"I got it from my father to buy a pair of gloves for the winter. I was up to see him this afternoon. But I don't need gloves, it's not my hands that need to get warm. I can always keep my hands in my pockets. I'd only lose a pair of gloves anyway."

"How come you didn't tell me? I mean we been sitting here dying of thirst – "

"I don't know. I guess I promised him I wouldn't drink the money..."

"Give it to me. I'll go up to Old Sal's and get a bottle."

"No, I'll go with you, I don't want to stay here, I'm sick of this room. I'd rather be out in the rain."

Ralph pulls the string on the light and opens the door. The hall is musty smelling and the only light is from the ground floor below. They walk by a shadow standing at the head of the stairs, they can hear the laboured breathing, one of the old men who lives in the house.

"This place gives me the creeps," Sully mutters going down the stairs.

Water is streaming over the street and the rain hits them like icicles. All the way up Water Street there isn't a soul in sight, it's like a ghost town. The wind whips the rain at them.

"Where we going to go once we get it?" says Sully. "We can't stay out in this." They walk along quickly with hands in pockets and shoulders hunched into the rain.

"We can sit in a boxcar."

"It's kind of cold."

"A few drinks and we'll be all right."

"Yeah."

§

The girl volunteered, nobody forced her into it. She was the zealous type, prepared to do anything for the good of the Party... The problem involved our middleaged and older citizens, they were in need of sex education and the girl said she'd do whatever had to be done... She wasn't too sure how her boyfriend would take it, but she reasoned: what was good for her lover must necessarily be good for all the people... She could hardly deny to others what she gave freely to him, not unless she was a hypocrite. As for him, he had no alternative but to like it if he was a sincere member of the Party.

*As a consequence of this correct reasoning —
along with her natural generosity — we find ourselves in
the wings offstage, and the auditorium is filled to
capacity with men and women mostly of the middle age
and what would formerly have been the middle class,
and from the way they're dressed you'd think they'd
arrived for a church service. They'd combed their hair,
pressed their clothes, polished their eyeglasses, they're
sitting stiff and solemn, there's scarcely a murmur out of
the entire crowd.*

*I've been peeking out at them, but I turn around
as the girl comes out of her dressing room — though
really, in this case, it could more accurately be called an
undressing room — because she hasn't got a thing on. She
looks sullen and peevish. The impression she gives is
unmistakable: she's doing this not because she enjoys it,
she'd rather not, in fact, but because of her ideological
obligation; it's her duty, you see...*

"Oh hell," she says. "All right, do we go on now?"

*"Anytime," I reply. "But I can tell you'd prefer not
to."*

*She hesitates. Obviously it's been on her mind,
she's been considering and reconsidering her decision,
her conscience has been in conflict with itself.*

*"No, you're wrong," she says at last. "It's perfectly
straightforward. I know he's out there, but we have to
share — everyone has to receive equal consideration —
there's no place for selfishness—"*

*While she's reassuring herself aloud I move closer
to her. I can't restrain myself, she's such a strikingly
pretty girl; she's barely eighteen and her figure is
magnificent, the likes of which I've seen only in the
movies and in magazines — and here she is — in the flesh,*

completely naked. My heart is pounding. I stand beside her, we're touching. I put my hand on her behind. She's real! It's not a dream — I can feel her — my fingers in the crevice of her lovely backside. I can't help it, my hand is on its own, nothing can stop it. I don't argue with it — my hand is right, it knows what it's doing! —

"For Godsake," she says. It's almost a groan. She's not all that pleased, but she doesn't try to stop me, she has to let it happen. I put my hand between her thighs, go right to the magic spot. "Damn it all," she says, but with a sigh of resignation, meaning, "What can I do?" Then she says, "Do you have to do that?" But I have no time for small talk. Her skin is cool, slightly damp, very young and smooth. My fingers play over her ass, revelling in the feel of her, my touch seems to be hypersensitive, it sends quivers all the way down to my feet —

"Well, I can't give to him — " meaning her lover — "what I deny others — " She's talking to herself.

"That's right," I agree.

She sighs and shrugs. "Let's go on."

The audience has been sitting there for a considerable time staring at an empty stage, but I detect no stirring, no murmuring, no signs of impatience. Peeking out again I see them waiting prim and stonefaced, in their Sunday best.

"I don't know what's been bothering me," she says, as we move towards the entrance to the stage.

Of course I'm naked too.

When we reach the edge of the stage, just as we're about to go on, she suddenly takes me by surprise. As though it's the most natural thing in the world to do she puts both hands around my staff, bends over, and backs onto the stage with it in her mouth — this is how we make our entrance! At midstage she straightens up. An astonishing change of mood has come over her. Her eyes are flashing. She smiles, and it's a lewd smile. "Was that nice?" she says. It must be the audience — the thought of performing before the audience must have excited her! Her eyes look deeply into mine; with gently seductive fingers she caresses me.

I'm breathing fairly heavily. "Oh yes... quite nice..."

I continue to make the most of things; this is my chance, I fondle her everywhere — what luck they selected me to be her partner! If you could see her, if you could touch her, you'd understand —

She turns her back to me and gets down on her hands and knees. Immediately I lunge at her face-first, I want to get my mouth right at her — but she says to me, her voice is trembling with excitement, "No, no, put it in, put it in — " So I do, rather I try to — I'm so hot and horny — I know I'm going to go off too quick. I climb at her, my lad hits her in the behind, it's groping for the right place, it feels something moist and soft and — down there and —

I can't hold it any longer —

POW!

But I've missed, I wasn't in, it shoots up her back and onto the nape of her neck, and the convulsion of the first great spurt causes me to recoil — and in lurching back I clutch her by the waist and pull her with me — and we go sprawling, me on my back and her on top of me, and the stuff is spurting and flying everywhere, it's all over the both of us, all over the stage — what a riot!

We lie there in a mess of semen laughing to kill ourselves —

And I take a glance at the audience — but to my surprise they're not sharing our hilarity — they're sitting solemn, sedate, sober, as though at church — they don't find it funny at all —

Except for one person who is on his feet applauding — her boyfriend!

"Bravo! Bravo!"

Only him, no one else.

"Wasn't that superb?" He exhorts the audience to show its appreciation, but he gets no response whatever.

But it doesn't discourage him, he remains cheerful, buoyant. He bounds up onto the stage and to demonstrate his enthusiasm begins nibbling on the girl's nipples...

The streetlight, as always, shines in my bedroom window all night. In its anemic purple and green light I see the face of Sullivan, livid and grinning. He's sitting on the chair beside my bed, bending over me and shaking me by the shoulder. I close my eyes again but he shakes me harder, whispering loudly, "Wake up! C'mon, kid, wake up!"

"Cut it out... I'm awake." I can hear my voice mumbling. "What do you want?"

"Wake up! Open your eyes!"

"Holy old..." This is all I need. I lean up on one elbow. I'm not happy at all, I'm a semi-insomniac and it really burns me up when my sleep is interrupted.

"What's going on? What are you doing here?"

"How's she goin'?" I catch the reek of wine right away. Sullivan's tongue is thick over the words. "You want a drink?"

I let myself sink back into the mattress, pull the bedclothes up around my ears, shut my eyes and say, "Are you insane? Get out of here."

"Come on, have a swig. I got nearly a whole bottle here. We got more in the car. Have a drink."

"I don't want any. Go on home and go to bed."

"Bed? What're you talking about? I can't go to bed, it's too early. What time is it anyway?" He reaches for the clock on my bedside table and holds it in both hands before his eyes, his head wavering from side to side as he tries to bring the numbers into focus. "I can't see the fuckin' thing. What's the time?"

I partially open one eye and squint at the clock.

"It's five to three. Goddammit! Get out of here. I have to get up in the morning, I've got an early class. Go on home, beat it."

"Five to three. Hm! Night's young, night's still a child. I can't go home."

"Well go someplace. Just go."

"Naw, I can't go home, the old lady'd kill me. Told her I'd be in by twelve. Who wants to go home? Nick's out in the car. I got him to stop here so I could give you a shot of wine."

"Don't talk so loud, you'll wake the old man."

He's got a bottle in his hand. He unscrews the cap. "Take a drink. It'll do you good."

"No, no, no. I told you I don't want any – get the hell out of here – I was good and asleep – if you don't get going soon I'll be awake the whole night–"

"That's okay. Come out with us."

"No sir. I don't want to. I have to get up early. I need some sleep."

He's silent a moment. "I thought you'd want a drink," he says. "Seems pretty funny to me... Didn't think I'd see the day *you'd* turn down a drink of wine – never thought that day would come – it's the first time—"

"Shh! Don't talk so loud, you're going to wake the old guy. You probably woke him already. Look Sully, I'm serious – will you get out of here so I can try to get back to sleep."

"Told you I can't go home. I already told you that."

"I don't care where you go. Nick's waiting for you, he won't wait out there all night."

"He'll wait. He better."

I decide to try ignoring him.

"You don't mind if I have a little snort myself?"

I lie there with my eyes closed.

"Eh? Okay if I take a drink myself`?"

I say nothing.

"Eh? You don't mind?"

His voice is rising. He shakes me.

"Eh? Okay if I take a small belt?"

"For Christsake." I lean up on my elbow again. "Take a drink, I don't care. But hurry up. I'm tired. I'm going to sleep."

He tips the bottle and the wine sloshes noisily down his throat. He lets out a contented sigh, slowly screwing the cap back on. "Sure you won't have one?"

I say nothing, head buried in the pillow. I'm conscious of him sitting there quietly for a while. Finally he says, "All right, kid, I'm gonna hit the trail. See you tomorrow." He gets unsteadily to his feet. "How do I get out of this goddamn place?" His knee smashes into the tin bedpost, it's like the sound of cymbals clashing. "Jesus Murphy!" He staggers along further, scraping against the wall. Beyond the light from the streetlamp it's black as a pit, I can't see him, but I hear him feeling his way in the hall. We live in a second floor apartment, the old man and me, which means Sully has to go down a steep flight of stairs to get out. I hear him descending cautiously, deliberately planting each foot. Near the bottom of the stairs there's an abrupt bend which fools Sully, he bumps into the wall, falls off the last few steps and goes crashing against the furnace pipe in the hall downstairs. All this I can tell by the noise he makes — I don't have to see him. There's a few seconds silence, then I hear him muttering a line of curses, he picks himself up, there's some more scraping and scuffling and the front door slams.

I know it's useless to try and get back to sleep. All I can do is lie here and hope that after an hour or so I might drop off. The old man must be awake too. Probably everyone in the whole building is awake, all four apartments, the way Sully hit that furnace pipe.

Fifteen minutes later, with my eyes wide open, I hear the downstairs door open and shut. And I don't have any doubts about who it is. I jump out of bed, turn the lights on, and when Sullivan comes into my bedroom I gesture for him to be quiet, pointing towards the old man's room.

"Sit down, I'll get dressed." It's the only way I'll get him out of here, I'll have to go with him. I was afraid he'd come back again. You can't talk sense to a drunk.

"Reason I come back—"

"Shh!"

"Reason I come back," he whispers, "is we picked up a couple of broads. Sure hide. Nick's been fuckin' one of them for months."

"Who are they?"

"Sure tail. Don't think you know them."

"I bet they're some lovely."

"They're not bad. Not the choice, but not too bad. Thought you might like to get your leather."

"Shh!"

While I'm stuffing my shirt into my pants he eyes the bed, where the sheet is turned down.

"Hey, what's that?"

"What's what?"

He points an unsteady finger at a large off-white stain on the sheet. I suddenly remember my dream.

"I don't know. Must've spilt something. Beer or something."

"Yeah, beer or something. Looks like pecker tracks to me."

"Looks like what?"

"Jizim. *Come*. Beatin' your meat in bed, eh?"

"You're nuts, Sullivan. That's the beer I spilt the other night."

"Sure. Beer. It still looks wet."

"Don't talk so loud. Don't talk at all. You already woke the whole house. Let's get going – and don't fall down this time."

"Can't see fuck-all in the dark. I almost broke my goddamn back."

§

The two girls are sitting in the front with Nick, and though Nick, as Billy Flynn once said, is thinner than a skunk's prick, you couldn't squeeze a blade of grass into that front seat with the three of them there. Sully was right, I don't know the girls, but I've seen them around and I know them by reputation. The one beside Nick is stout and solid and muscular, built something along the lines of a heavy draft horse. She comes from a little place in the woods called Semiwaugen, which is what Nick calls her, Semi-waugen, or Semi for short. The other girl is known as Big Jane, and you don't need to look twice to see why. She's about double the size of Semiwaugen.

Sully and I get into the back and Nick drives off.

"Where we going?" says Sully.

"Gravel Pit. Can't drink here," says Nick, "the cops drove by twice already. They got their eye on us."

Big Jane looks over the back of the seat.

"Aren't you going to introduce us to your friend?" she says to Sully.

Sullivan informs them who I am. I perceive that Semiwaugen is giving her attention fully to Nick, snuggled in tight to him, but Big Jane bats an eye at me. I don't know what to think. She's not what I consider my type, my preference runs to girls about a quarter her size. Something tells me I'd better get prepared.

"Pass the wine," I say to Sully. I up-end the bottle and lower the level a good three or four inches.

The streets are all empty at this time of night, and we pass through a sequence of shadows and streetlamps, down corridors of elm and poplar trees still with their leaves, past houses closed up for the night. Everything's asleep — where I should be. We reach the edge of town and head out along the old Williston Road and drive for about a mile through the woods until we come to the Gravel Pit. It's like a labyrinth of great gouges in the ground. We turn in and bounce our way as far as the third or fourth pit so that we're well hidden from the road, and Nick shuts off the lights and motor. For a second it's still and peaceful. I look out the open window; it's not a cold night, the sky is cloudless and there's a glowing half-moon. The sky is dazzling with stars.

"Give's a smoke, Nick. I can't find mine," says Sullivan.

"Ain't got none. Only got a couple left."

"Have one of mine," says Big Jane, reaching back a pack.

Because of the moon and stars it's not as dark as it might be. I can see Big Jane's face clearly. She tells me to take a cigarette too. "Go ahead, dear, don't be shy."

It's not very long before the air is rank with the smell of smoke and cheap wine and cheap perfume. There are a couple of quarts of wine going the rounds at once. The first one that comes my way I really give it a guzzle, I open my throat as wide as it'll go and the wine sluices down like it's coming from a hose. I keep taking big drinks whenever I get my hands on a bottle — I've got some catching up to do, I'm way behind the others — and I'm not suffering from over-confidence. I've got a suspicion what might be on Big Jane's mind and if it comes down to it I don't want to look like a bumbling idiot, or a reluctant one. Big Jane keeps talking to me, looking over the seat and giving me the old eye. She raises her arms above her head and stretches. I'm getting the effect of the wine by now, so I catch her by the wrists. She laughs and arches back over the seat. She's pretty supple for such a large girl. She's arched over so much – and I'm feeling loose by now – I plant one on her lips, an upsidedown version. Her mouth is open and her tongue starts rummaging around. I change the position of my hands, reaching them down and getting a grip on her by the tits. Sully snorts.

"Drive 'er, b'y!" he says. It's a wonder her spine's not dislocated, she's bent backwards like a bow. After a minute or so I release her and I see Sully's chuckling to himself.

"No sweat, eh?" he says. "Eh? What do you say? No sweat?"

He says this at the top of his voice.

"Show a little tact," I say to him.

"What do you think, Jane? The lad's got 'er made. That right, Jane?"

"It's none of *your* goddamn business," she says, but not bad-humouredly.

The wine keeps flowing. The next things that happens I'm tugging at Big Jane and she's doing more than her share to help – I could never manage it alone – and she comes tumbling over the seat and into the back and lands on Sully like a ton of bricks.

"Come out!" he hollers. "For fucksake!"

He puts one hand between her legs and the other on her tits so he can push her aside. "You nearly flattened me."

We're squeezed into the corner and my hands are on the move, under her bra, down her jeans, I'm putting the feel in everywhere – she doesn't complain, it suits her fine. The wine has done wonders for my confidence. It's only my second time or will be if we go the distance, but I can handle things. It's time to move, strike while the iron's hot.

I whisper in her ear, "I want to... to... uh–"

She whispers back, "To what?"

"To fuck you!" Never mind the poetic language, not at a time like this – it's down to the basics –

"Okay," she whispers. Only she adds, "But not here. Later."

She's said okay! I feel my blood racing.

"Why not now?" I don't care who watches.

"No. Not here. I don't want to here. Later."

"You're just saying that."

"No I'm not."

"How do I know you mean it?"

"I give you my word. I never break my word. When I say a thing I mean it."

"What'll we do later?"

"We'll fuck."

Oh boy.

"Good. That'll be good."

"Yes."

"Where?"

"We'll find a place."

In the meantime Nick has been fiddling around with Semiwaugen, and Sully's been darting little feels at Big Jane, and peeking over my shoulder to get a look at her ass or bare tit or whatever happens to be showing at the moment. During all this the wine continues to go around. A hand shoots up from wherever it's occupied and grasps a bottle, you hear a gurgling noise, then the bottle moves on.

All of a sudden Nick shoves Semiwaugen aside and squawks, "Enough of this bullshit. I gotta get me skin. I'm getting too jeezly horny."

"Right!" I feel like an old hand at the game. "Where'll we go?"

"Not our place," says Big Jane.

"Why not?"

"Our old bag of a landlady – she don't want us bringing guys in."

"She won't hear us," says Sully.

"She'd hear you, that's for sure. You never shut your mouth."

"Fuck 'er then."

"You fuck her yourself."

Nick cackles. "Just your speed, Sullivan."

"I don't give a shit. I'll fuck anything. Bring her on."

"Go way, Sully," says Big Jane. "You never got a piece in your life."

She gives my tool a little squeeze.

"Ha! Dyin' old Jesus, I've taken more tail than the whole bunch of yez put together."

He gets a great horselaugh for that.

"You wouldn't know what to do," says Big Jane.

"You think so, eh? You get this big root into you, you'll know. You'll be going around with eighteen broken ribs."

"Where'll we head for?" says Nick. Then he says, "I know," and starts the car.

"Where to?"

"Billy Flynn's. That crazy-arsed bastard's alone, he's got a couple of beds in that shack of his."

§

"Don't tear 'er down, b'ys, I'm coming."

Billy Flynn opens the door and we stampede in. It's not much of a place, hardly bigger than a doghouse. With no partitions the entire house might equal one normal-sized room, but it's divided into two little bedrooms and a room that serves all other purposes: kitchen, living room, dining room, smoking room, bar and toilet — represented respectively by a bucket of water and a hotplate, a couch with the stuffing coming out, a small table and a chair, a full ashtray, a half-empty quart of Hermit wine on the table, and a slop and shit bucket in the corner.

It took a bit of banging on the door to get Billy out of bed. He's pulled his pants on in a hurry, the fly's undone and the braces he wears over his winter underwear are all twisted. He's in his bare feet. Billy is forty or fifty years old. Fidgeting with his braces to straighten them out he says:

"Didn't know who it might be at this hour of the night. For a minute there I thought it was Arnold. Couldn't of been, though."

Billy used to share the shack with an old drunk by the name of Arnold McGrath. This Arnold was in his customary condition one afternoon — the past summer, only a few months before — he was sitting on the Station Wharf working on a quart of wine, there were some kids swimming there, and for a joke they pushed him over – and he never came up, not until the next day when they found the body.

"We want to do some ridin'," says Nick in that squawky voice of his.

"Oh. Well... whatever you like. I'm still half asleep. Have a seat. I've got a little bit to drink here."

"We got lots of wine," says Sully. "We sold a couple of tires today."

He's holding a bottle in each hand.

"Shutup, Sullivan," says Nick.

"What's wrong with selling tires?" says Sully innocently.

Instead of doors Billy's rooms are closed off by two dirty old blankets hanging from the ceiling. Not being a man to squander time Nick puts both hands on Semiwaugen's back and propels her through one of the blankets, toppling her onto the bed on the other side. "Get your drawers off," he says. "I ain't got all night." He then kicks off his shoes and climbs out of his pants and disappears behind the blanket, still wearing his shirt, shorts and socks. There's about a two second interval before we hear a heavy thump! thump! thump! thump! like the bed's jumping up and down on the floor. Sully looks at me. "Oh Jesus," he says. He begins laughing, and he can't stop – it's like he's been hit by some form of hysteria – I know by the look of him, I've seen him like this before, you couldn't get him stopped even if you cut his head off, not for a while anyway. In the tiny bedroom Nick and Semiwaugen are galloping up and down and every so often Nick lets out a whoop followed by a cackle.

"Drive 'er b'y!" hollers Sully, tears in his eyes.

"Come on," says Big Jane, tugging at my arm.

"Wait'll I have another drink, just a second." While I'm gulping down a bit of wine she goes behind the other blanket. Sully points a finger at me — now he's laughing at me. I put down the bottle and slip behind the blanket.

The second bedroom is slightly larger than the other one, there's just room enough to stand beside the bed, about a foot of space along the length of the bed. Big Jane is sitting there so I sit beside her and put an arm around her, or halfway around her, as far as it will go. She's not fat, she's just big; if she were a man she'd be just right for a football linebacker. She looks very good to me right now — she hasn't got such a bad-looking face; feeling the way I do, sailing along on a bellyfull of wine, I wouldn't ask for anything better —

"Well... Let's get at it," I say.

She takes her blouse off and unbuttons her jeans, and while she's doing this I get out of my shoes and pants — and leave on my shirt, shorts, and socks. You can see I don't miss much — I kept my eye on Nick so I'd know the procedure. You've got to learn from those who know.

Prying my knob out through the fly in my shorts I take a safe from my wallet and roll it on.

"Help me with these." She's trying to get her jeans off. I catch hold of them by the cuffs and pull. She's pushing down on them around her thighs and I'm pulling, but the damn things seem to be stuck on her. "Wait, I'll get them," she says.

She works on one leg of the jeans and after a resolute struggle succeeds in getting one leg off. Then she slides her panties off one leg, lies on her back, opens her arms, opens her legs, gives me a sly look, an inviting little smile, and says, "What's the hold-up?"

She still has her bra on, as well as half her jeans and panties, but that seems all right, since I've still got on my shirt, shorts and socks. It's not what I'd daydreamed about, but if that's how it's done, that's how it's done. "Take this off, anyway," I say, my hand on her bra.

"You take it off."

"Okay."

Except it's easier said than done, the truth being that I haven't undone all that many bras in my day. In the end she does it herself, nimbly reaching both hands around behind her and unhooking the thing. I shove it up above her breasts — and that's where it stays, shoulder straps still on.

Being on top of her is something like lying on the crest of a hill, overlooking the world; there's lots of room and not too much fear of falling off unless I crawl too close to the edge. After pawing her breasts a while and giving the nipples a little mouth work I conclude it's time to get to the business at hand — But I find it's not so easy. What with the french safe and the drinking, and mainly my lack of experience, I'm not all that sure how the fellow's doing — it's up and willing, but is it in or isn't it in? It might as well be frozen for all I can feel it. I'm poking around thinking it must be in by now — but I can't really tell. How are you supposed to know? Better make another stab, I think. I back off and attack again. There — that must be it, it must be home. Time to start the bed-thumping. You don't need education for that. I start going in and out like a rabbit — and I'm at it a while when I begin to sense something's not quite right. I try to sneak a look but I can't see that far. I slide one hand down and — dammit! Just as I feared, it's not in place at all, I've been going up and down on her belly.

Thank God I'm half-drunk. I try to pretend I know what I'm doing, I hope she'll think I do anyway, something different, a new kind of preliminary playing around. There seems to be only one solution — I take hold of the weapon and then try to shove it in by hand — but I can't find the place. I'm starting to sweat, I don't want to look bad.

All this time Big Jane isn't saying anything, but finally she gets impatient; she bats my hand away and grabs hold of my rod and puts it where it belongs herself.

After that I don't have to do anything. She starts her great hips going and I just hang on. I go bouncing up and down and it's not long before we're both panting and snorting and the bed's banging against the wall — and I can still hear Nick and Semi thumping away in the other room—

The blanket opens and Sully peers in at us laughing to kill himself —

"Get out of here, Sullivan!" I say.

"Oh Jesus..."

His face disappears and the blanket falls to.

Some time later — this is it, away I go — I burst off into the safe — but I'm too soon for Big Jane. She doesn't stop, she's only begun, she keeps on tossing me up and down until I think my balls are going to explode. It becomes quite painful — it's time to stop, to relax — it hurts like hell to keep on — but she won't stop. She's got me by the ass heaving me in and out —

"Hold 'er, that's enough," I gasp.

She subsides. She mustn't have noticed I went off – or if she did she wanted to drain me dry –

I lie on her panting for a while, then roll down off and remove the safe – and wonder what to do with it – it's all wet – maybe it broke – it's a wet mess of rubber and jerkins – I don't want that in my hand – I flip it under the bed.

Big Jane is smiling. Now that it's over I'm in pretty good spirits myself.

I get my clothes on and go into the other room. Billy's just coming in the door from having a leak, buttoning his fly. I see that Sully's all finished laughing. About the same time Nick emerges from the hanging blanket and starts pulling on his pants.

"Okay, Sullivan, now's your chance," he cackles.

"Are you crazy?"

"What's the trouble? Don't you want your skin?"

"I got some taste in broads. I'm not like you two bastards, I don't fuck every scrag that comes along."

"Go on, you're chicken, Sullivan."

"Do you think I'd go after one of you fuckers? I got some respect for my cock. You don't catch me taking seconds."

"Go 'way, Sullivan, you're just chicken."

"Bite me arse."

"Give her a try, Sully." I nod at the room where Big Jane is. "It's great stuff."

"Naw, I ain't in the mood."

Later, when Big Jane and Semiwaugen come out, it's like being in a crowded elevator. Nick says, "I'm going way the hell home, it's past my bedtime."

"What's your rush?" says Big Jane. "It's still early."

"It's early all right. The fuckin' sun's coming up. Any of yez want a drive come on, otherwise you can walk."

"We'll walk. It's not far." Big Jane's sitting beside me on the couch, leaning against me. I'm feeling kind of smug about the fact I just got laid.

"Suit yourselves."

"I'll come with you, Nick," says Semiwaugen.

"What's wrong, you got legs, ain't you? The walk'll do you good, take some of that beef off." With a last cackle Nick goes out the door.

With him gone there's a little more breathing space, but not much. The rest of us sit around drinking up the wine and having a smoke, and Semiwaugen says to Billy, "What've you been up to lately, Billy?"

"Oh, you know, Semi, I haven't been doing all that much, not since last winter. I've been laid up a bit with the ulcers or something, the stomach gives me a turrible time. I was in the hospital about a month ago."

"I didn't see you there." Semiwaugen and Big Jane both work in the kitchen at the hospital.

"No, I only stayed a few days. I had to get out, they wouldn't feed me. All they give me to eat was a bit of porridge and a couple of soft-boiled eggs and the odd glass of warm milk. A man's not going to survive on the likes of that. And I couldn't get a drink at all. The doctor there, he tried to tell me to cut out the drinking altogether, he said it was bad on my stomach, and that's why I was throwing up blood. I don't know where they get these new doctors – from the jungle, I think, over there in Africa. This one was blacker than a new hearse. I didn't figure he could do me any good. You know I don't eat all that much anyway, but when I do I like a good feed of meat and potatoes. Oh, it's a turrible place, that hospital, they don't pay no attention to your needs at all, you could be dying of thirst in the middle of the night and they won't do a thing for you. I asked the nurse, I was getting kind of dry during the night, and I asked the nurse to ring up Bumpy Brown – on the quiet, you know – she looked like a nice girl – and ask him to bring me a quart of wine – the taxi driver, Bumpy Brown – but she wouldn't hear of it. Give me a big rakin' on top of it all. I got lost in that place too. You can't tell one room or floor from the other. I woke up in the morning and climbed out of bed, I thought I'd go down to the pond to have a wash–"

"Down where?"

"Well, you know, where they have them sinks and things, there's a room there with bathtubs and toilets and such, so I went hunting for this place. I asked some old bugger limping around half-dead, I asked him where it was, they showed me earlier but I forgot, you see, and he said it was down a few floors and you turn left and then right and up this way and down that way, and so on, so I went wandering off in my nightshirt with my arse sticking out the back – and I never did find the place. After a spell I got tired of looking so I figured I'd head back to my room. The only thing was I didn't know which way to go. I didn't even know which floor I was on, because I'd been up and down so many different stairs I lost track. I didn't like to look too stupid, you know, so I never asked none of the nurses or doctors to help me out, I just walked around like I knew where I was going thinking I'd run across my section sooner or later. But it's a big building, that hospital. I must've spent four or five hours wandering about like a goddamn fool in my nightshirt, I was at it the whole morning, looking into doors and peeping around corners. I might still be prowling around there if it wasn't for a nurse from my floor finding me and leading me back. But I didn't stay long. Soon as she was out of sight I got into me clothes and made straight for the stairs and went all the way down to the cellar and asked the first nurse I saw to show me to the door. I knew there was a door down there, I've walked by it many times on my way past the hospital. Course I still got the bad stomach, I never got cured in the time I was there — but that can't be helped. I'm not able to do much work, but then I never was much to work anyway, even when I was healthy. All I did last winter was a few weeks in the woods cutting pulp. That's a hell of a job, it's freezing cold and you're up to your arse in snow. And we had only the one chain saw, a real old one, the first one they made, I think. Ben Sweeney was with me, he borrowed the saw off Harold what's-his-name, Harold Bevan, and when we come back Harold asked Ben how the saw was. Ben says to him, 'Oh, it's a fine saw. It's so dull it wouldn't cut the cock off a snowman.'"

§

When the last of the wine's gone, Sully says, "Let's get going, the old lady'll be getting up soon."

"You're not leaving already?" says Big Jane.

"We'd better shove off," I say.

"When'll we see you again?"

"I don't know. One of these days."

"Don't call him, he'll call you," says Sully.

"Yeah, I bet."

I feel all in — it's been a long night — I let out a big yawn. "We'll see you later. Thanks, Billy."

"Okay, boys, come anytime," says Billy. "I don't have much company with Arnold gone."

Outside it's broad daylight, a fresh new morning, still early enough that the streets are empty. The sun is shining and the birds are up and chirping. It seems a shame to go home to bed but I can hardly keep my eyes open. As we walk we don't say much. In a couple of minutes we reach Sully's street and he says, "I'll see you this afternoon."

"Sure." I'm supposed to go to classes this morning but the hell with them, I'd never keep awake. "Wait—"

"What?"

I'm curious. "Listen, how come you didn't take a crack at Big Jane? You were acting pretty funny there."

"Oh. Well, I couldn't."

"Why not'?"

"Well, there was Billy's coat hanging there—"

"What?"

A sneaky grin comes over his face. "When you were in there banging her I had to do something. There weren't enough broads to go around. When Billy went out for a leak I put the hand to 'er. So I'd already got off, see? Right up Billy's coat sleeve. It wasn't bad — I've seen worse looking sleeves."

§

If some stranger asked Sully his name he was told, "Sullivan. Just call me Sully?"

"Yeah? What's your first name?"

"Sully, I told you. Hey, did you shit your pants, I smell something funny around here."

"What? I don't smell nothing." Sniff sniff.

"Yeah? Maybe it's the pulp mill. Do you know Mick Whelan, he comes from near your place..." etc.

Sullivan's first name was Percy, but the only people who used it were his parents and anyone who felt like provoking him, either out of malice or just to see him react. But it was folly to exchange insults with Sully, he could always give back twice what he received.

Sully's old man was named Percy. For a middle label they gave him his mother's maiden name, Winfield. Percy Winfield Sullivan.

"That was a great practical joke to play on a kid, eh? hitting him with those tags. Percy! Purse for short. They might as well have called me handbag. And Winfield. That's a great name. They'll be going around calling me Winnie — Winnie the fuckin' Poo."

If you heard this: "How's she goin', Percy?" you were likely to hear something like this next: "You still ridin' dogs, fartface? Danny Moar said he caught you fuckin' that big Saint Bernard of his."

Sully said one day, "When I get the Jesus out of this hole you'll never hear any of this Percy Winfield stuff again, I'm changing my name."

"What to?"

"Rico. Rico Sullivan. How's that sound? Pretty nifty, eh? I always like Rico, there was a guy in a movie called that, some cowboy movie. I never forgot it."

"How about a middle name?"

"I don't need one. you don't need a middle name. I could use something ordinary, Johnny or Dave or Jack, something like that."

§

Sully didn't read much. I tried different times to get him to, but it was no use.

"I started to read a book once," he told me, "I forgot what it was, but I had it there, I was really gonna read it, only I picked it up the wrong way — you know, with the pages down, and the words all fell out on the floor. I didn't know what order to put them back in so I just swept them up and dumped the whole lot in the waste basket. That's true."

§

The back porch of Sully's house smells of fuel oil, where they keep their tank for the kitchen stove. We follow Sully through the porch into the kitchen, Ralph, Harris and myself, and there's Mrs. Sullivan in her apron, a thin, busy, bespectacled woman who gives the impression of never having laughed in her life — sarcastic, fussy, a compulsive house cleaner. Ralph feels out of place, a middleaged man with us young fellows; he averts his eyes, shuffles his feet, says in a loud over-formal voice, "Nice day, Mrs. Sullivan!"

"Yes, it is." Her reply is cold; she doesn't deign to so much as glance at him.

"C'mon," says Sullivan impatiently, and we follow him up the stairs. It's an attic-type upstairs, the sloping sides of the roof forming the walls. There are two rooms, the rear one containing a couple of brokendown chairs, a bedspring, some trunks and boxes full of old clothes and things, all stacked in an orderly way. The two rooms are divided by a short hallway, just long enough to accommodate a closet on each side of it.

Sully produces the wine bottle and passes it around, then hides it under the pillow on his bed, opens the window and we climb out onto the veranda roof. It's one-thirty in the afternoon, a mild pleasant fall day for a change, with the leaves on the maples starting to turn red. Sully has a small radio with an extension cord, and he brings it out onto the roof with us, and we sit against the wall listening to music. The Everly Brothers are singing *Let it be me*.

"Aw... I shouldn't be here with you guys," says Ralph. "I don't think your mother's too crazy about me."

"The hell with her. She knows what she can do."

"That's no way to talk about your mother, Sully."

"What the fuck."

"If it wasn't for your mother..." Ralph's voice trails off. "Aw, I don't know..."

"What?"

"You wouldn't be what you are today."

"Yeah, that's it."

"No, but you're supposed to respect your parents. That's one of the Commandments." Ralph is quite serious.

"The old man was telling me last night, about this Bobo Kelly," Sully says, "you know that half-witted guy from the East End – he told me this last nightabout – about when Bobo was twelve years old or something, he picked up a cat off the street and tried to sell it. He was going around knocking at all the doors, and he came here and the old man answered. Bobo's holding this starving cat in his arms, and you know how he talks, he says, 'Wanna buy a titten?' The old guy knows what he's saying, only he pretends not to. He says, 'Buy a what?'

"'A titten. Titten. Wanna buy a titten?'

"'I don't know what you're talking about. A titten? What's that supposed to be?' You know what the old man's like, eh? always agitating.

"'Titten. A titten.' Bobo's holding this cat up, trying to pass it off as a little kitten. 'Wanna buy a titten!'

"'I can't understand you,' the old man says.

"Bobo gets right mad – He looks the old man in the eye and says, 'Look, mister, you wanna buy a doddamn tat?'"

It's really a lovely day – it's almost like summer, you could take your shirt off it you wanted, it must be Indian Summer. In July Sully was out on this same roof for a few days in his bathing suit, and after the second day he started bragging about the tan he was getting.

"I don't see any tan," I said to him. "Roll your sleeve up."

We both rolled our sleeves up and I put my arm next to his and it was much darker – he's naturally more fair-skinned than myself.

"Well," he said, "I mightn't have too much of a tan on the arms, but on the whole... on the hole I'm pretty brown."

Another song comes on the radio, it's quite popular, by Tommy Edwards, and it's not a bad song so we listen to it. When it's over Sully sings a few lines of it – he's got a pretty fair voice – only he rephrases the words this way. Instead of *I can't love another, I still love my first love*, he sings:

"I can't love another,
I cornhole my brother–"

He says that's "The William Bryenton song", referring to the eldest of two brothers who live across the street in a big yellow house.

"Talk about your fruits," he says.

"I heard that," says Harris, "but Jesus, I mean, it's bad enough, but jeezless brothers."

"That can't be true, Sully," said Ralph. "You shouldn't put stories like that around."

"It's true all right, they're queerer than a couple of three dollar bills."

"I heard of brothers and sisters, but I dunno... two brothers," says Harris. "They must be fuckin' sick."

"You better believe it. Not only that, he's always coming over here to whack off."

"Yeah?"

"Sure. He's watching us right now, he keeps an eye on the house so he'll know when the old lady goes out shopping. Then he comes over. He'll phone me up, or he'll come across the street and knock on the door, and he'll say, Sully, can I go up to your room and read? Mummy's vacuuming and it's too noisy at my place. Only when he gets here he don't read, he's too busy pounding his pudding."

"How do you know?" says Harris.

"I seen him. Lots of times. He don't try to hide it or anything. I'm getting sick of seeing him with his fuckin' hard-on, beatin' off all the time. He don't give a damn. I just ignore him."

"Go on, you're making all this up," says Harris.

"Yeah? You don't believe me all you have to do is watch him yourself."

"Watch him? How am I gonna do that? I'm not gonna watch him! Anyway, it ain't true."

"Okay, so you don't believe me."

But Harris is curious. We crawl in the window and have another drink, and when we're out on the roof again he says, "He really comes over here and pounds off?"

"Almost every day."

"Go on."

"I told you, I seen him, lots of times I walked up the stairs and there he was, right in the act, pumping away for all he's worth."

"What's he say?"

"Oh, he'll say something like, 'Sully, go away, can't you see I'm busy?' At first he tried to come onto me but I let him know I'm no fuckin' fag, I give him a punch right in the mouth. You talk about your hard-on going down fast. He started bawling and crying and saying everybody hated him, and he liked me and he thought I liked him, and how it wasn't his fault the way he was. He might as well be dead, he said, and he was crying away. You had to feel a little sorry for the fucker, I suppose it's not his fault — if you were brought up in a house he was you might be a fruit yourself. Anyway, I told him not to bug me, to get his clothes on and get the hell home. He called me about a week later and said he was sorry about what had happened, and would I let him visit my place again, come over and read, he promised nothing would happen like the last time. So I said okay, only if he fucked around with me again I'd really let him have it next time."

"I wouldn't let the bastard do that in my place—"

"What the hell. He gives me a couple of bucks every few weeks. He gives me his allowance. I told him first to stay clear of here, but he said, 'Jeepers, Sully' — that's the way he talks, see — 'Jeepers' — he says, 'Jeepers, Sully, don't be so mean. I've got a present for you.' I thought he was going to say something that might earn him another rap on the chops, but he says his old man gave him a buck, and since I'm his dearest friend he wants to give it to me. Of course I never refused, but then I had to let him use my room — it's sort of like rent money. They keep a sharp eye on him at his place, his old lady's got an idea what they're up to, him and Lawrence, so she's always opening the toilet door or the bedroom door and looking in to see they're not jackin' off or cornholing each other. So William needs a place to go. So what, eh? I make a buck or two a week, let him pound off all he wants. I just tell him not to get it over my bed 'cause the old lady'll think it's me. He brings his own rag with him, he's been using the same rag for years, the thing's almost alive."

Ralph is shaking his head at hearing all this. We all know Sully is notorious for inventing stories, everyone knows it. "I'd hate to think you're talking about William like this if it's not the truth," he says.

"Like I said, if you don't believe me all you got to do is see for yourself. The old lady's going shopping this afternoon. You watch, he'll be over here if he thinks I'm alone. All you got to do is hide."

"Where, under the jeezless bed?" says Harris. "He knows we're over here."

"That's easy taken care of. You can all look like you're leaving and then one of you double around the back. You can hide in the closet. He'll never see you."

"I'm not going to do that," says Ralph. "I might be crazy but I'm not that crazy."

"Okay, but don't say I'm lying then. Put up or shut up."

"What do you think?" Harris says to me.

"You know Sully — You'd better see it with your own eyes."

"Why don't *you* hide in the closet?" Sully says to me.

"Not me. Harris can do it. He's all curious—"
"He's too chicken," says Sully.

"I ain't chicken. I'll do it."

"Holy sufferin'! Let's have another drink of that wine."

§

In a while we see Mrs. Sullivan come out the yard and head down the street to do her shopping.

"He won't come over till you're gone," says Sully. "Here's what to do. We'll wait a bit longer, then the three of you get up and leave. I'll be at the window and you yell up at me that you're on the way to the tavern, and for me to come down when the old lady gets home. He'll hear all this, see, he's over there now, hiding behind the drapes, and he'll hear us — and I bet a million bucks he'll be over in five minutes, once he's sure you're not coming back. But here's what you do, Harris, soon as you're down to Butler Street cut round through Mills's yard and go across the field and over our fence and in the back door, and I'll hide you in the closet. You can peek out through the curtain. He won't be able to see you."

"I don't know, Sully. He's liable to spot me."

"You can't back out now."

"He'll see me for sure."

"No, he won't. Once he gets going he don't see nothing, only his knob."

"Jeez, I don't know..."

"You didn't believe me, now's your chance to find out."

"Give me that last drink."

"Hey—"

"Give it to him, Sully, he needs the extra courage."

Harris polishes off the bottle. "What the fuck, I don't give a goddamn," he says. "You're just giving us a lot of shit anyway. I'll find out. But I ain't staying in that closet too long. If he don't come over–"

"Don't worry, you'll get your show."

§

Harris is dumbfounded, shaking his head all the way down the street. He laughs, then makes a gagging sound – We can't get anything out of him, we're all eager to hear what he saw – spying on William –

"Holy old dyin'..." That's as much as he'll say.

"C'mon, Harris, what happened? Tell us about it."

"Holy old... You shoulda seen him..."

"Don't say I didn't tell you," says Sully.

We're only a short way from Memorial Park, and when we get there we sit on a bench by the bandstand, with Harris trying to collect himself. He's the centre of attention, it's a new experience for him – he loves it – he's in no hurry – he's got something we want, so he holds onto it. He's still thinking of what he just witnessed, it made a big impression on him. At last he stops exclaiming and relents – "Okay, okay" – he'll tell us. He lets his story out, taking his time – we're all ears –

"I done what Sully said, I circled round and got in the back door without William seeing me, and then Sully put me in that closet upstairs, right, Sully? He shoved me in that jeezless little closet and I could hardly move. I was sitting on a clothes hamper or something where I could see out through the crack in the curtains. I sat there a minute... I thought Sully was just trying to make an arse out of me, leave me waiting there for an hour and nothing would happen and he'd have a big laugh about it... I was only gonna stay a minute or two and then get up and leave... That's the kind of thing you'd do, Sully — eh, you guys know him—"

"C'mon, get on with the story."

"I felt like a fool sitting in a closet, so I got up and went to the head of the stairs to listen, and I heard the door open and Sully talking to somebody. I ran back and got in the closet again — And then I heard someone coming up the stairs and the next thing William went walking by into Sully's room. I nearly shit, he was only two or three inches from me and when he went by — It's a funny feeling — you'd swear the guy knows you're there, cause he's so close — but he didn't see me. It'd be jeezless embarrassing, caught in a closet like that. Anyway, he went by and I didn't know what he was up to, and I didn't want to stick my head out to look, so I just waited, listening. After a bit I could hear these squeaking sounds, like the bedsprings going, I knew he must be on the bed. I pulled the curtains aside and sort of eased my right eye out — I was afraid he'd be facing my way, but he was lying on his stomach on the bed with his clothes off — balls naked — and his arse was pumping up and down like he was riding some plug — I thought he was riding for sure, I couldn't see too well, it was the first thing occurred to me — that he'd got some slut in there and was fuckin' her – she'd come in the window or something. I kept looking, then I saw he was all alone – he was riding the bed – the blankets! He almost caught me cause he got up all of a sudden and I was off guard, but I hauled my head in just in time – but I thought he had me, I could hear his bare feet trotting across the room towards the hall – but he kept going by, right in front of my eyes, no more than two or three inches away – Holy Jesus, boys..."

"C'mon, Harris, keep going."

"You should've seen him, he had this big hard-on and he was jackin' away for all he was worth – really going at it. He went into the other room, then came galloping back still pulling on it, he run back and forth like that half a dozen times before stopping in Sully's room. I never even thought, I just stuck my head out to see what he was doing in there. He didn't notice me – he was fumbling around, he had this old rag that was all stuck together and he got it opened and then he started pumping like mad with the rag on his cock – his eyes bugging out – jerkin' a mile a minute – Jesus!"

"Go on, Harris, go on–"

"Fuck – I almost puked – he went off in the rag and took it and started licking the stuff up. He ate it all, all that jerkins, swallowing it like he was starved. I nearly threw up, so help me Jesus. I pulled my head back in and put my hand over my mouth so I wouldn't puke – I'd seen enough of that – eatin' the stuff!"

"What happened then?"

"That was all. He got his clothes on and walked by, and all this time I was trying to keep from sneezing or coughing. I practically held my breath the whole time while I was in that closet. When he was gone I come out, and talk about cramped, my muscles all stuck together – I'd hardly moved or breathed. You'd never think, eh? That innocent-looking little fucker – serving mass all the time – gonna be a priest – wouldn't say shit if he was up to his neck in it – pounding off all over the place – and eatin' it!... It just goes to show..."

§

It wasn't long before that story was all over town, with Harris telling everyone he ran into, as though he'd never whacked off himself. It was good for a laugh. And Sully had already been telling the world about William and his brother Lawrence – dressing up in their mother's clothes when she was out – and the rest – all the details – He could fill in the whole story – about them buggering each other –

William was a student at St. Timothy's, in the same year as myself, in fact. When he'd walk downtown, say past the Castle Restaurant where there was usually a gang of loafers sitting on the steps and holding up the wall, someone invariably would holler, "Hey William, how about a blowjob!" Or, "Where's that old rag of yours – Maloney here's thirsty!"

I was hanging around there myself one afternoon when William came along with a bag of groceries in his arms. When he was just past us some guy yelled out, "Hey William, you wanna suck my prick?" Most times he pretended not to hear these remarks, but they must have been getting to him, which wasn't surprising. He stopped, and I saw he was close to bursting into tears – He had a hard time controlling his voice – He said, "You leave me alone! I never hurt you! You have no manners – or anything – " But that's all he got out, the bunch by the restaurant started hooting and laughing. He turned and walked quickly away towards home.

§

Sully was like Little Red Riding Hood. His mother was trying to get him to go visit his grandfather in the old people's home – Mount St. Matthew –

"He'll probably want you to get something at the store for him. And take this raisin bread I baked."

"How come I'm the only one who ever has to go see him? How come you or the old man don't go?"

"Please don't refer to your father as the old man. I've told you that. I suppose when I'm not around you call me the old woman."

"Naw... the old lady."

"I don't know whatever happened to your sense of respect – if you ever had any –"

"As I was saying –"

"Because your father and I are busy, he's out working every day and I have the house to take care of, we never have a free minute."

"He's got lots of time on the weekends."

"There are things to do around the house, which you ought to be doing, but you're too busy running around with those drunks and good-for-nothings you hang out with."

In spite of his protests Sully didn't mind visiting his grandfather, he liked the old guy. He only went on that way so that next time he asked for money it would appear they owed him something.

Mount St. Matthew was only a few minutes walk from Sully's, up beyond the church and the elementary school and adjacent to the Hotel Dieu Hospital. It was a large building of roughcut stone with front steps climbing to an arched double door — but this wasn't where the old men were found. Through this door you came to a chapel and the priest's quarters, a TV room for the priests and nuns, a lavish guest apartment for visiting Bishops and the like, and on the floors above private rooms for the more well-to-do old people. Sully's grandfather was staying in one of the dormitories in the basement with five other old-timers. The basement was honeycombed with these crowded dormitories, cubicles set off by makeshift plywood walls and with the beds pressed so close together they were almost touching.

We walked in through the ground floor door — the service entrance to the building — and were met by a strong odour of dirty underwear and stale tobacco and some unappetizing smells from the kitchen which was also located in the basement. Lines strung across the rooms were hung with washed sheets and pillow cases and articles of clothing. There seemed to be a space problem at the Mount — at least in this part of it—

"How're you feeling?" Sully said to his grandfather. The old fellow was over eighty but lively and good-humored, not at all senile. He was tall, slender and white-headed, and there was a bright alertness to his eyes.

"Good! Good!" He was a little hard of hearing and tended to talk emphatically, as people getting deaf do. "Come out in the hall here, where there's some room!"

It was only mid-afternoon, but two of the beds were occupied by old men, the sheets pulled up to their chests. They must have stayed in bed all the time, these two, unless they liked to hit the sack good and early. A man fully dressed was sitting on a third bed staring out the ground-level window.

"Did you get out today?" said Sully.

"No! It was too cold!" said his grandfather. "I don't wear my winter underwear up here. I can't, it's too warm inside." There was a steamy uncomfortable heat in the place, something like being in a laundry. Probably there was a laundry in the basement as well.

A small old man with a pyjama top tucked into his pants approached us, where we stood by the hall door, his feet scraping along the gray cement floor and one arm held taut at his side. You could see he had a partial paralysis. The way he walked, with his arm held like that – Sully's grandfather said to him, "Where're you going? You looking for a fight?" The little fellow had his arm cocked as though ready to let go a haymaker, it was frozen in that position.

"What?"

"A fight! You looking for a fight?"

"Oh. A fight! Yeah! Do you want one?"

"Sure! Let's step out on the grass!"

They laughed. Then they began talking about the man sitting on the bed, the one looking out the window in a trance.

"What's wrong with him?" said Sully's grandfather. "He got me to help him out of bed this morning. Can't he help himself?"

"I don't like that old bastard," the other man said. "I wouldn't help him. I don't know, maybe I'll be like that too, one of these days... maybe so. But I wouldn't ask someone to help me sit up."

"Who was that yelling last night?"

"What?"

"Who was doing all the yelling last night? Woke me up, right in the middle of the night!"

"Yelling? What yelling? I don't know."

"What was he saying?"

"I don't know. I didn't hear anyone. I slept all night."

"I couldn't figure out what it was. Sounded like French."

A younger man on crutches and with a cast on his leg came along, carrying two packages of pipe tobacco. He handed them to Sully's grandfather along with some change. "That's right, ain't it?" he said.

"Yes, yes, that's great! You get around better on those crutches than most people do without them!" The man grinned dully, obviously retarded. The hospital had probably stuck him in the old folks home to recover from his broken leg before returning him to the "Poor House", as the County Home was known.

"Here, take this!"

"Oh." The fellow on crutches accepted a quarter from Sully's grandfather, muttered thanks, and whirled around on his crutches and left us.

"Well, listen, boys!" the grandfather said, after Sully had told him we were in a hurry and had to leave. "When you come up tomorrow don't forget the pyjamas. Size thirty-eight. How much do you think they'll be?"

"I don't know."

"I'll give you the money now. What does a pair of pyjamas cost these days?"

"Well... I guess four dollars would be enough."

"All right. Four dollars." He took the money from his wallet and gave it to Sully. "This is enough now?"

"Yeah, I think it's just right."

"Don't forget. Size thirty-eight. And pick out a good colour!"

"Sure." Sully stuffed the bills in his pocket. "I'll bring them up tomorrow."

"Okay, and don't forget! I need them."

"I won't. We'll see you tomorrow afternoon then."

Sully and I left the Mount and took a shortcut across the lawn past its *Keep Off The Grass* sign, plowing through the newly fallen yellow and brown and red leaves as we went.

"Well," he said, "here's two forty pounders of wine."

"How's that? How'll you get the pajamas?"

"Charge them in the old man's name." He meant his father. He called his grandfather gramps. "The old man never goes up to see him so he won't know. I'll tell him gramps wanted pyjamas but didn't give me any money for them."

§

We got Roger Allain to go in for us. He was sitting on the steps of the Post Office across from the Liquor Store watching the world go by, getting up every so often to put the tap on someone. Roger was a young wino, a prodigy you might say, only a couple of years older than Sully and me, dark-skinned and unshaven, his hair oily and hanging in his eyes. He had the indifferent, quietly furtive look of the older panhandlers, the patient single-mindedness —

I'd noticed him a few days before this, as I was walking along Water Street. He was coming around the comer of Martin's Clothing Store, emerging from the alley that leads to the tracks and the river. It was a cold blustery day and he had on a heavy coat and a pair of army boots with gray socks rolled down on them — and no pants — his bare legs stepping along like a pair of scrawny sticks, pale and bruised and spindly. As he went by me I could smell the wine off him.

"Roger, you'd better get some pants on," I said.

"I'm gonna buy a pair," he murmured.

He strolled along the sidewalk with heads everywhere turning. I decided to tag along behind and see what happened. He went into Martin's and made straight for the pants rack. A girl came over to him, one of the clerks.

"I guess you're looking for a pair of pants," she said.

"Yes. I need a new pair of pants."

The other clerks exchanged glances, grinning, holding back laughter. The store manager appeared, immaculate in a tie and sports jacket, and said, "Yes sir, what can we do for you?"

"He wants a pair of pants," said the salesgirl.

"I thought so. Okay, let's see what we can find."

I thought they'd throw him out, but I guess if he had the money it was as good as anyone's. He did odd jobs from time to time.

"How about these? Here's a nice pair of jeans. What size do you take?"

"Thirty-two. No, I don't want jeans."

"You don't want jeans?"

"No, I don't want them. I don't want jeans. I wear dress pants."

"Dress pants. All right, sir."

"Size thirty-two."

"What happened to your other pants." ·

"I ruint them."

"You ruint them?"

"Yes, I ruint them."

"How'd you do that?"

Roger didn't answer for a moment. "I just ruint them."

"Okay, sir. How about these? These would look very good on you."

He held them against Roger, a quite smart-looking pair of woolen check pants.

Roger was slow to make up his mind. He held them against his waist, gazed down at them, considering.

"Are they thirty-two?"

"Yes, they're thirty-two. Try them on."

Roger didn't move, he was still appraising the pants.

"Come this way, sir, there's a fitting room over here."

He took Roger by the arm, and Roger said, "Okay," and raised one foot and tried to get his boot off.

"No, not here, you can do that in the fitting room."

The manager led him away.

"Well, that's one way to go shopping for a pair of pants," remarked the salesgirl. "You don't have to bother carrying your old ones home with you."

We were in need of Roger's services, to go into the Liquor Store for us. In those days you had to be twenty-one to make a purchase and neither of us was, as the clerks knew. In fact you were supposed to be twenty-one to get into the tavern, but nobody bothered you about that. Roger was the man we came across, sitting on the steps of the Post Office. He had on his new pants, though they didn't look so new now; they were barely recognizable, torn in places and stained with mud.

"Get us some wine, will you, Roger?" said Sully.

"Sure." He held out his hand for the money, looking up and down the street. "Go round behind the Post Office and wait for me there. The cops caught Pat Carey last week and give him two days in jail."

We went behind the Post Office and waited.

"The son of a bitch is liable to run off on us," said Sully.

"Yeah, he might. I'll go take a look."

I went to the corner of the building where I could see the Liquor Store door, but we needn't have worried. Roger came out and made directly for us.

"Here you are, boys," he said, thrusting the bag of wine on us, leaving his hand open for the fee. Sully gave him a quarter which Roger slipped quickly into his pocket, looking the other way.

"Where'd you get the sharp pants, Roger?" said Sully. I'd told him about them while Roger was on his errand.

"Oh. I don't know — I don't know where in Christ I got them. I woke up in the bushes the other morning and they were on me. I can't figure where I got them. I hope nobody don't come asking for them back. They're brand new. I hope I didn't steal them."

"You bought them," I said. "At Martin's. I saw you."

"Yeah?" He looked down at his pants. "Maybe I did. I had some money the other day... I thought I lost it. Hmm." He walked away, thinking it over.

§

They were milling around the streetlight in front of the restaurant like moths.

"Hey, Robinson, you got a quarter? We're trying to get a bottle — we just need another quarter. Okay, give us a dime anyway — What's a fuckin' dime? Thanks. You're all heart. We'll do the same for you some day."

"There's Dearborn. He should be good for a touch." He was coming out of the narrow alley beside the restaurant with something under his jacket.

Sully collared him. "C'mon, give us a drink — don't be so cheap."

"It's only beer," said Dearborn. "It's just a quart of beer, it's all I got."

"We got nothing against beer."

The three of us ducked into the alley, clear of the light from the streetlamp and the red-and-green blinking of the Castle neon. Sully tipped the bottle and kept it there, gurgling away until it occurred to Dearborn that he wasn't going to stop. He pulled the bottle away. "Hey, don't kill it, don't drink the whole damn thing."

"Beer, beer, it's good for the heart, the more you drink the more you fart." Sully demonstrated the truth of the jingle and got a small chuckle out of Dearborn. Dearborn kept a closer eye on me, in fact he kept his hand on the bottle when I put it up, and I barely got a taste before he drew the bottle away. "There's almost none left," he said.

"We'll give you a drink of wine later," said Sully. "We nearly got enough for one now, we just need another quarter. Lend us a quarter, will you."

"I don't have a quarter. Honest to God, I'm broke."

"Yeah, yeah. Give us a dime then."

"It's my last dime, all I got is a dime."

"A dime's no good to you. We'll give you a good belt of wine when we come back from the boot's."

With Dearborn's dime and a final cruise around the booths in the Castle we brought our total up to two dollars, the price the bootleggers charged for a quart.

Dearborn was waiting outside by the door.

"I'll come with you," he said.

"No, wait here," said Sully. "Sal won't open the door if there's too many."

"Make sure you come back."

"Don't worry." When we were up the street Sully said, "He donates a dime and thinks he owns the bottle."

There were at least half a dozen bootleggers in town, but the one we'd been patronizing lately was Sal's place, a couple of blocks from the Castle — a dilapidated shack with a sagging roof and weatherbeaten shingles. The yard was dark and the blinds were pulled. It was only when we were close that we could see chinks of light coming through the blinds. To get in the house you had to go through an attached woodshed which was kept locked by a wooden bar across the inside of the door. Sully beat on the door. It was pitch dark in the yard. There was no response so he pounded harder. When still nobody came he hollered, "Sal! Open up! Sal!"

"Who's there? Who's making all that fuss?"

We looked up and saw a shadowy head poking out one of the second-floor windows. The voice was a woman's but it was deep and coarse as any man's.

"It's me — Sully!"

"Oh. Is it you, Sully?"

"Yeah, it's me."

"Why didn't you say so?" Sully was a favourite of Sal's, he knew how to tease her, make her laugh, they got along real well. "Who's with you?"

"A friend."

"Who is he?"

Sully told her who I was. I'd been there almost as many times as Sully but it never seemed to register with her. She said, "I don't know him."

"He's all right," said Sully. "He's been here with me before."

Whenever I showed up alone or with somebody else the only way I got admitted was by saying I was a friend of Sully's and that he'd sent me to get a bottle.

Now I think of it Sal reminds me of Cookie — the way Sullivan got along with those old lady wino and bootlegger types.

"C'mon, let us in, we can't stand out here all day, we'll get cold," says Sully.

"Just a minute. I'll be right down."

There was a substantial delay before we heard the inside door open, then feet on the shed floor, then a fiddling about with the bar and a clump as it was set aside, and the door opened. "Come in, hurry up. Bolt the door after you." I put the bar back on and followed them into the kitchen.

There was another woman in the room, Sal's companion, they'd been sharing the house for years. The other woman's name was Old Sam, or so she was called. I never heard her speak, she just grinned and blushed if you addressed her. Both women were around fifty. Old Sam's skin was heavily wrinkled and looked as fragile as toilet paper, and she had an odd way of walking, as though her feet had been bound as a child, the way the Chinese used to do. Every step she took appeared to hurt her. Sal was much stronger looking. She had a leathery face and missing front teeth, and one eye turned up in her head so that only a part of the iris is visible. What she looked like was an old pirate.

Sal's father was also in the kitchen, a man in his seventies; he was sitting on a couch with an enormous paunch hanging down between his knees. His nose was the size and shape of a potato, but pitted with holes more like an orange. There was an open quart of wine at his feet. He didn't look at us as we came in and didn't say a word while we're there – nor did Old Sam, as always –

"How've you been keeping, Sully?" says Sal.

"Not tea bag," says Sully. "You're looking good tonight, all dressed up."

"Oh, I'm not dressed up at all, this is just an old thing I wear around the house."

"I thought you were going out to a dance or something."

"Dance? Me? Ha ha! I've never been to a dance in years. Don't talk so foolish, Sully."

"I thought I seen you at the dance last Saturday – you and Sam – I never knew you could jive like that, Sam."

Old Sam blushed and averted her eyes, and a faint sound escaped her. She pressed her lips tightly together, coyly disapproving.

Sal laughed heartily.

"You wouldn't have seen us at no dance, we're too old for that kind of nonsense."

"Go 'way, Sal. How old are you? You can't be more than thirty-three, thirty-four."

This was the kind of attention she liked to get, and Sully could have gone on with it all night. Only we had to get moving, we couldn't stick around forever. I cut in to say we were in a bit of a rush, someone was waiting for us, so Sal dispatched Old Sam hobbling up the stairs, getting both her feet on each step before attempting the next and leaning her arm against the stair case wall. It was several minutes before she returned carrying a bottle of Hermit. I stuck the bottle in my belt, and when we were leaving Sal followed to bar the door behind us. "Be careful going out the yard," she said. "The Mounties were parked across the street by the garage earlier. They might still be around somewhere. Don't let those bastards catch you."

"We'll look out for them."

"You can take the back way, go down the station way."

"Yeah, okay."

"Come again, Sully. Anytime."

"Don't worry."

We waded through a patch of raspberry bushes behind the shed and climbed over a leaning snow fence and went down an incline and came out near the tracks. There was a raw east wind coming off the water, gusting against us as we crossed the open ground towards the freight shed. At the corner of the shed there was a tin-shaded night light and it trembled and rattled, the shadows beneath it dancing crazily. We climbed up onto the loading platform and walked down a line of boxcars until we found one open. Inside we sat down out of the wind and cracked open the bottle.

"What time is it, anyway?"

"I can't see. It's too dark. Light a match."

"Wait'll I get this butt rolled. No sense wasting a match."

"Pass me your makin's."

A smoke always felt good after a shot of wine. By the light of the match we saw it was only a quarter to ten. We still had a good jump on the night.

"Where did Ralph disappear to? I saw you talking to him."

"Him and the Bishop went sneaking off somewhere. Maybe the Bishop's got a gallon hid away."

"The Bishop wants to be careful." He was on a two year suspended sentence now – that's what they gave him for stealing the Volkswagen, the one he rolled over in the ditch. He used to be a notorious altarboy at Mount St. Matthew, very officious and saintly. Nobody liked him then, not even the nuns after a while; they'd doted on him at first, with his sanctimonious airs, but he overstepped himself, strutting around like the Bishop himself, giving them orders. They kept their eye on him and one day found him wearing the priest's alb and chasuble and pacing the floor with his hands clasped talking to the ceiling in Latin. They kicked him out then, figuring he was half-cracked. A few years later he started drinking, you'd run across him and he'd have a gallon of mass wine with him, that he stole off the nuns. He knew their routines, when they'd be at prayers, where the wine was kept. He'd slip into the vestry and make off with a gallon. It was a risky business, mixing theft with sacrilege, but it didn't bother him. If you mentioned it he'd look gravely down his nose at you — "*In troibo ad altare Deum*," he'd say. "*In nomine Patris, et Filii*" — and so on, blessing the gallon. Never a smile, solemn as can be. He had the Latin memorized, out of the missal, with no idea what it meant, most of it.

Sully and I sang a few songs and talked about Toronto, the wine warming our spirits — the wind beating against the metal sides of the boxcar —

"When you think of it, we had a pretty good time up there," said Sully. "Not that we knew it then — But once you're back here—"

"We were crazy coming back. We could've got work if we'd tried."

"Well, we tried some."

"If you'd only gone for that painting job — You had it — You were hired — All you had to do was show up."

"I couldn't help it. You were supposed to wake me."

"I did — but you went back to sleep."

"I don't remember."

"Well, I woke you. You said you were getting up."

"I must've been talking in my sleep. Remember that handbill place, eh?"

"That was something!"

We'd stayed awake the whole night, and at seven in the morning walked several miles to a fenced-in yard lined with panel trucks, their backs to a ramp, loading stacks of circulars. They needed five hundred men every morning, according to their ad. The truck bosses picked their hands out of an impressive crowd of derelicts. There were five hundred and three men there that morning, including us, and at the end there were only three not selected – Sully and me and an Indian from Northern Ontario. That did a lot for our job-hunting confidence. It was worse for the Indian, we didn't care that much, we were so sleepy we just wanted to get back to our room and go to bed. We still had a little money left, and gave the Indian fifty cents. He didn't have a thing, he'd been trying for weeks to find work, a young fellow. He was going to have to go back to his Reserve, he said. They'd told him nobody would hire an Indian, and he'd found out for himself it was true. He didn't ask us for the money, we were just in a sympathetic mood, having seen what it was like, everyone getting picked but us, every kind of bum and wino. We put it down to our beards, such as they were. You might as well have had leprosy as a beard in those days. *Beatnik*, you'd get called. That's all changed with time, of course, but it hadn't then.

"Where's that bottle?" Sully said. All I could see in the dark was the tip of his cigarette, when he took a drag on it. I could hear the wine bubble down his throat. "The old man's at me again," he said. I felt the bottle nudge me, got a hold of it and took a drink. "Him and the old lady, they're both at it, going on about what a worthless son of a whore I am – they haven't stopped for a week. Telling me all the things they done for me, working themselves to the bone – just for me – the ungrateful bastard that I am – the disappointment of their lives. The old guy said if I didn't get work soon I'd have to get out. I told him that suited me fine, I was sick of the company around there anyway. The old lady howling... It gets on your nerves.

All the chances they give me, every opportunity in the world, how they would've put me through college but I was too lazy to even get through high school — hanging around with the town drunks — no offence meant — Why don't I dress decent and shave that goddamn beard... The old beard's coming right along, eh?"

"Yeah. Another few months and you'll be able to see it."

"It's thick — it's growing good. Because it's blonde it don't stand out too much. But it's better than those couple of strands you got going there. It looks like you glued a few junks of thread on your face."

"Huh! At least you can see mine."

"You watch — another week or so and I'll look like Ralph. The old lady's right down on it — She don't have no trouble seeing it. And get a haircut, and look at those boots — Jesus, she never stops — shine those fuckin' boots. Somebody told her, said they seen me in the window of the Castle when I was supposed to be at mass — She figures now I do this every Sunday. I mean, I do, but I had her fooled — I'd ask someone who was there which priest was on the hill, McCarthy or Malley, and what the sermon was about — But now she don't trust me. If she's not yapping about that it's something else. It's all the time now — don't stay out late, get up earlier, bring in the oil — take a mechanic's course — that's another thing they're on, I'm supposed to learn a trade — go to the dentist, take a bath, stop swearing — paint the shed, mow the lawn, feed the cat, eat your dinner — make the bed — clean your room, take the garbage out, change your socks — drinking again! — They were quiet for a while, but now they're started back at me... You're lucky your old man's not like that."

"Yeah, he doesn't say much. It's too bad this boxcar wasn't moving right now."

"With our luck it'd stop in Clifton."

When the bottle was finished we left the tracks, heading up towards Water Street. I felt myself staggering some – but I didn't mind it – staggering, swaggering. Sully let out a long whoop – "Fuck 'em all," he said.

§

A coke glass full of wine at one of the booths, a stiff drink from someone's pint in the washroom, the restaurant jammed, a packed house, the air choked with smoke, shouts, screeching laughter, the jukebox pounding in the background – I can't find Sully, I've lost him, I drift up and down the aisles with my head swimming. It's Friday night – that's why everyone's there – I reel around, looking for something to happen, caught up in the energy of the place – looking for I don't know what – a girl, a friend, an enemy, another drink, feeling powerful, unrestrained, potential. I make for the door. There's a horde of bodies swarming around out there too. I manouevre towards the door, waitresses squeezing by, elbowing and kicking their way down the aisles with glasses of coke clutched in their fists. I pull the door open, there's a guy in a Navy uniform facing me, he's coming in, I'm going out. "Outa my way," he says, kind of snarly. I stay put. "Fuck you, Jack." I don't give it a thought. "I said outa the way!" The neon light blinks on him, his face is ugly, his mouth twisted threateningly. There's a crowd around him, on the steps, the sidewalk, milling under the streetlight on the corner. The scene is frozen, suspended, everything's stopped while I reach back and uncork a right. It catches him in the mouth, he staggers back and goes tumbling down the steps to the sidewalk, a startled look on his face. I realize what I've done — there's no walking away now, see you later — I'm in it now. He comes up on his feet and I reach him in one bound and we're both swinging for all we're worth, wild haymakers, roundhouse rights and lefts. I don't feel it when he hits me, not a thing, I'm busy swinging like a windmill, anaesthetized by the wine, he's wasting his time. I connect with a good one, square on his chops. He backs off, then he charges, he wants to wrestle. We go down in a heap and I slip free, I'm sitting on him, piling the fists to his head. He tries to swing back but he's underneath, at my mercy. I take my time, hit him repeatedly. I can sense the crowd around us, feel them, I'm conscious of being encircled, the restaurant's emptied, must be a hundred spectators — two hundred — we're on the sidewalk at the main downtown intersection. Cars stop to see the action. Roars of excitement, shouts of encouragement. The sailor's struggling at me, it's getting hard to hold him down, he's slippery, strong, desperate — and I feel guilty, holding him down and slugging him — like the bad guy in the movies. I spring to my feet, jump clear of him. "Get up, you cocksucker!"

Roaring like an ape — full of fight —

He's on his feet and swinging widely again. I skip out of the way, he misses, misses again, almost falling on his face — the crowd cheers. I shoot in with the left hook, he takes it on the nose, counterpunches — but I'm out again, he's swinging blindly, bleeding from the nose now. I dance around, circling him, another left hook — smack! — roars from the crowd — they love it — He looks worried, fagging out fast. I tag him another one, he's too slow, he can't read my left hook. We're about the same size, we're both boozed-up, it's a fair scrap. I'm exhilarated, primitive, pitiless — a human face to pound, to hammer back at. I don't care if I get hit — I'll hit him harder. I smack him again, trying to flatten him, but he won't drop. I fake the right, then throw the left — then fake the left, throw the right — it gets him every time! I hit him at will, but he's stubborn. He wants to quit, he's beat, he's had it, but he won't go down — he holds on — that's all he can do —

"You had enough?"

He's finished, bleeding from the forehead, the nose, but he won't say it. I tag him a couple more. His legs buckle. Enough? He nods. But I'm not satisfied —

"Get down on your knees!" I don't know what I'm saying — I must be crazy —

The crowd cheers — "Hit him again, let him have it!"... "No, no, he's had enough, break it up"... "Kill the fucker!"

Meanwhile I'm roaring at the guy, like a maniac, ready to plow him another one. He won't do what I say... "No," he says. But he's beat.

There's a sudden diversion in the crowd, they're opening up. I look aside. A car with a flashing light. I didn't notice it pull up. It's too late, two big cops come through, a hand on my shoulder..." Okay, you guys, come with us." They've got the both of us.

"What for? We're just fooling around... it's nothing serious..."

"Yeah, yeah, we know. Let's go."

The sailor's face is streaming with blood, his whole face. Nobody seems to know him, but he's from Bannonbridge, he tells me later. He's been away for a long time. One of the cops looks at him, then at me. "Pretty good with your fists now, aren't you?" he says. He's picked me up before. There's approval in his voice. He sees there's some good in me after all...

§

At the police station the sailor washed his face, got most of the blood off it, and they emptied our pockets.

"Put them in separate cells and lock them. We don't want these two going at it again."

"Nothing to worry about," I said, "we're all through fighting. It was only a little tussle, we've got nothing against each other. Right?" I was feeling benevolent – it was easy –

The sailor managed a wry smile. "Sure, it's all over."

But the cops weren't convinced. They took us down to the row of cells in the basement and locked us in. Before the cop with the keys left the sailor told him again – he'd told them upstairs already – that his leave was up and he had to catch the train for Halifax in the morning in order to get back to his ship – it was leaving Sunday morning for the Caribbean –

"You should've thought of that earlier," said the cop. The two of us would have to appear in court Tuesday, he said.

"But I can't. I have to get back."

"That's tough."

"I *have* to." The sailor pleaded – he was quite distressed – I thought he was going to break down. Altogether he was having a bad night.

"I'll pay the fine now, I don't care how much it is–"

Slam! The big steel outer door closed behind the cop.

"The rotten bastards," I said.

"I have to get back to my ship or I'll be in real trouble, I can't wait around here till Tuesday–"

There wasn't much room in my cell but I walked up and down the few feet that were available. There was a wooden bench for a bed, a block of wood for a pillow, a moth-eaten gray blanket, an iron toilet in the corner, like a large rusty flower pot, with a well of black water below. The walls were painted dull brown and were rough enough to have been hacked out of natural rock, like a man-made cave. In the common room outside a lightbulb glowed dimly – it stayed on all night, keeping the cells in twilight. The place reeked of carbolic disinfectant. I was still keyed up, it took me some time to relax, going over the bout in my mind, weaving again, bobbing, swinging – The funny thing is, I'd belonged to a boxing club when I was thirteen, it was where I learned to box, and our volunteer instructor was a Mountie!

I wound down eventually. I was tired enough, I'd drunk quite a lot. I lay on the bench after a while and smoked a cigarette.

"What's it like in the Navy?" I called out, but the sailor only mumbled something in reply, I couldn't make out what he said —

§

Around six in the morning I heard them letting him go, as they'd meant to all along, after making him squirm and sweat through the night. He had to post bail, the same sum as the fine and court costs — fifteen dollars altogether for creating a public disturbance. It was a standard procedure. When he failed to show up before the judge the bail would be forfeited.

Nervous and grateful he hurried away to catch his train — and in a few days he'd be in the Caribbean, cruising in the sunshine. I wondered if I should join the Navy. Sully and I tried to get on a freighter once, down at the station wharf, but they told us we had to belong to the Seamen's Union, and there was no such thing in Bannonbridge.

When he was gone the cop opened my cell so that I had the large outer room to myself; there were no other prisoners, it'd been a slow night. But I was still behind the big armored door.

"When do I get out?" I asked him.

"When we're ready to let you go."

"You let the other guy loose."

"That's right. He had a train to catch."

"What's so special about him?"

"Nothing."

"So why can't I go too?"

"Because we're not ready to let you go yet."

"When will you be ready? What time?"

"You'll find out."

Slam! The heavy steel door closed again.

I wasn't feeling all that fit, now that I was up. My head was humming, my mouth dry, foul-tasting, my stomach uneasy. I noticed the skin was barked off my knuckles.

There was a row of dusty barred windows high up on the wall and flush with the ground outside. One of the windows was raised to let the air in. Around eight-thirty a couple of kids came along and squatted at the open window with the morning sun streaming in behind them.

"Hey, mister, what ya in the lock-up for?"

"Nothing. It's none of your business."

"Tell us."

"Get out of there. Beat it."

"What'd they arrest you for? You steal something?"

"No."

"What?"

"For fighting."

"Yeah? Who with?"

"I don't know. Some guy."

"Who won?"

"Nobody."

"Somebody musta won—"

"Yeah, I betcha the other guy did."

"No, he didn't."

"How long they gonna keep you there?"

"I don't know."

I went into my cell where they couldn't see me and sat on the bunk. They kept looking in, crouched, faces against the bars, but after a few minutes they got tired of it and left. Then I went out and began pacing up and down again. An hour or so later I head a rattling at the door – but it was only the janitor. He asked me if I wanted a cup of coffee.

"Okay. I might as well."

He locked the door again, and then minutes later came back with a large white mug of black coffee, and said apologetically, "I couldn't find any milk, it must be all gone. But there's sugar in it."

"This'll do fine."

"Did you have a good sleep."

"Well, not bad, considering. It's not much of a bed."

"No, the mattress is pretty hard." He looked at the windows with the sun filtering through the dust. "It's a nice day," he said. "The radio said rain but it don't look like rain to me."

"When do you suppose I get out of here?" I asked.

He shrugged. "I don't know. You'll have to ask the corporal."

"When will he be around?"

"Oh... I couldn't really say. He should be back before long."

"I guess I'll have to pay a fine."

"I guess so. I don't really know much about it. Fighting, was it?"

"Yeah."

"You'll likely have to put up bail."

"Bail?"

"I think so. Of course I don't know for sure."

"Balls." I was hoping they'd just let me go, and I'd try somehow to scrape up the fine money by Tuesday, when I'd have to be in court. But now they'd have to call up the old man. He'd already bailed me out for drunkenness twice in the past month or so. You couldn't blame him for getting fed up.

Around two in the afternoon I saw him peering in the window at me. "Yes, there you are," he said. His voice was trembling.

"Hi," I said. Like I'd just met him on the street.

"You goddamn..." That was the extent of it. He posted the bail, almost half his weekly pay cheque. Not another word.

In a way Sully was better off, the way he went about life. I don't think he ever felt much guilt about anything.

§

On Tuesday morning I made a brief appearance in court before old Magistrate Peterson who looked bored and half-cut. I pleaded guilty, was fined twelve dollars and three dollars court costs, and that was it for my bail money, or I should say the old man's bail money. Then I went home and cooked the dinner. After dinner I lay down and read a while. Then I went to an afternoon class. When I got back I found Sully sitting on my bed, wearing the charcoal-gray suit his mother had bought for him — the first time I'd seen it on him — and a white shirt and tie. Just inside the door was his suitcase.

"Travelling somewhere?"

"You're goddamn right," he said. "Are you with me?"

"What going on?"

He got up off the bed and walked across the floor, then back again and stood by the window, looking out.

"I told them, you bring a fuckin' priest around here and that's the last you'll ever see of me. I'll be gone so fast you'll think you never had a son. They kept saying they were going to do it. Where's your makin's?" He rolled a cigarette and lit it. He sat down, then got up again. He was very fidgety. "The old man told me Sunday he'd found me a job, eh? painting again, and I was supposed to be grateful, I was supposed to show up at seven-thirty in the morning ready to work. All arranged, he said. Well, I told him what to do with his job, I'm not gonna be no fuckin' painter. I already tried that scummy trade. I told him I'd get a job when I was ready — I didn't ask the old quiff to find me work. What's he think he's running anyway, an employment agency? You should've heard the two of them, they were set to go at me till the sun came up, I had to get out." He stopped suddenly and said, "You got anything to drink around here? I didn't get a chance to make it to the Store yet."

I told him I had nothing. "So what happened?"

"Well, like I was saying, I was beating it out the door and the old man yells after me, 'I mean this, Percy, you be there tomorrow ready to work — or else!' Yeah, sure I'll be there. Just don't tell the foreman to hold his breath. I didn't know what he meant by that 'or else!' Anyway, I headed down the street and I started to think about the situation, like I wondered, you know, if maybe it wouldn't be such a bad idea to work a week or two, not too long, eh? just long enough to get a few bucks together and then fuck off again to Toronto or somewhere. Save every cent of my pay, not blow it like last time. Two weeks work and I'd have enough for the both of us, you and me, right? Well, anyway I landed at Ralph's place – any port in a storm, like the man said – and who do I find there with him but the Bishop – and he's got one of those big gallons of mass wine. I was going to go and get you, but by the time we were done saying hello and how's she goin' and all that there wasn't enough left to make it worth your while. That Bishop's off his fuckin' nut. You remember – you probably don't – Friday night when we lost track of each other, when you got in that fight – I didn't know where you went, I was looking around when I spotted Ralph and the Bishop bolting down the street and it looked like the Bishop had a big watermelon under his coat. They were just lucky the cops didn't come along. I took off after them and got a couple of cracks out of what was left of the gallon. The Bishop wasn't too drunk – he could hardly see. When the jug was empty he left us, he said he was going back to the convent for another one. He figured they wouldn't be checking the closet till next morning and since they'd miss one gallon just as easy as two he might as well get his mitts on another one while there was time. Anyway, he got it all right, and he must've saved it, hid it somewhere, because there it was Sunday in Ralph's room with the two of them going at it. Well... to make a long story short, despite my good intentions I was in no mood to get up at six o'clock Monday morning and go out painting all day, feeling half-sick like I was. There's a lot of wine in a gallon. I mean, I would've called you but there's no phone in that dump where Ralph lives. And I couldn't leave, you know those guys, they'd of took off before we got back.

"Anyway, in the morning I told the old man to get the fuck out of my room and stop trying to wake me up in the middle of the night. There was a big row, and the old lady was into it, screaming and howling. I had to crawl way down under the blankets and plug my ears till they went away. Then I went back to sleep. That was yesterday. Well, today about one-thirty I was just starting to wake up when the old lady comes in the room and says, 'Percy, there's someone here to see you.' I figured it must be you or Nick or someone. 'Get dressed and come down,' she says. 'And right away.' She won't say who it is, but I don't like the tone of her voice. I get up and go downstairs and who's there sitting in the living room like he owns the place but Father McCarthy."

The Parish Priest — not the first man you'd want to meet first thing in the morning, even if it was early afternoon in Sully's case —

"He looks at me over his glasses," says Sully, "you know the way he does, giving me the old evil eye, and he's got that expression on his face like he's ready to kick the shit out of you. 'Sit down,' he says — Not hello or good morning or how're you feeling — just 'sit down.' I'm supposed to collapse in a chair shaking with fright. But I'm not feeling that way. I say to myself, 'fuck you, ya old quiff' — and out loud I say, 'How's she goin', Father, nice day, ain't it?' And I don't bother taking a chair like he told me, either. I didn't invite the

132

son of a whore around and right off the bat he's trying to tell me what to do.

"'What can I help you with today, Father?' I got my comb with me and I'm standing there combing my hair, and I'm still sort of half-asleep and the old stomach's not A-one. I don't feel too much like entertaining visitors, especially not that sour-looking cocksucker. And I've got a few things going through my mind... like the old lady – I'm more than a bit pissed-off about her bringing him down here –

"McCarthy takes his time opening his mouth, he's still trying to nail me down with that stare, like a rattlesnake – that's what he looks like – but it's not working. I put my comb away and roll a smoke and stare back at him for a while, until finally it's getting too much so I give him a big wink, like he's a queer trying to give me the eye. That's all it takes to get him going, he turns two or three colours and says, 'You must be the most insolent disrespectful young pup in this entire town –'

"'Flattery will get you nowhere, Father,' I say.

"'If it weren't for your parents – I wouldn't be bothered, I wouldn't waste my time. I really can't understand it, they certainly don't deserve the likes of you for a son.' He holds it there a minute with his lips clamped together, giving me the glare over the top of his glasses again.

"'Well, Father,' I say, 'if it's not one thing it's another. If they didn't have me to worry about it'd be something else. You have to look at in the right light.'

"'How old are you?'

"'Me? Christ, I don't know. I never thought about it. You could ask the old lady, she probably knows.'

"'You left school — you reached grade nine, didn't you? How long ago, four years, was it? You're twenty now and you haven't done one tap of work in those four years, you're running around the streets drunk all the time, you don't go to church, you won't take a job when it's handed to you on a platter, you've got no sense of responsibility — you're just a source of trouble and anxiety for your mother and father. Why don't you take a look at yourself, consider what you're doing, what you're coming to–'

"'Yeah, maybe I better. There's a mirror in the bathroom — just a sec.'

"I have to take a leak anyway, so I go have one and come back, and I say, 'I'm looking pretty good, Father, maybe not the best-looking guy in town, but I could be worse — like some people I know.' Beside his ugly mug anyone'd look good. 'What you need,' he says, 'what you should've had long ago — is someone to take you out behind the woodshed and give you a good whaling — then you might learn the meaning of respect– '

"'We don't have a woodshed, Father, we burn oil, but you're welcome to try it anyway... By Jesus, just name the place.' I mean who's he think he is, anyway, eh?

"'I wouldn't soil my hands on the likes of you,' he says.

"I laugh at him. 'That's a real funny line, Father. You're a natural comedian. You should be on the stage. There's one leaving in ten minutes – if you hurry you might catch it.'

"I'm not lying," said Sully. "It's all true. I didn't give a goddamn. Soon as I walked in the room and saw him I said to myself, this is the last straw – I'm hauling the hell out of here – packing my bags and going. Old McCarthy got hotter and hotter under his white collar – Nobody ever talked to him like that before. He says, 'I knew this would be a waste of time – trying to talk sense to a-a-a-' He got so worked up he started stuttering – 'a wise-guy, a smart-aleck little punk – that's what you are – you think you're clever but you're not – I've seen your kind before–'

"'Where was that, Father?'

"'On the front street – hanging around the Liquor Store – bums – begging for money – bothering people – that's where you'll wind up, with the rest of them–'

"'Sounds great. And I know your kind, too. You should be in the fuckin' pen, the whole lot of you, instead of picking pockets every Sunday. A bunch of jeezless con-men – Do you ever think of working for a living?'

"He jumps out of his chair like he's gonna take a swing at me – he's all steamed up – and I'm set to duck and lift him an uppercut, but he doesn't try anything – he just says, '*I beg your pardon!*'

"'That's okay, Father' – I'm keeping cool, like I'm humouring some idiot – 'We all let a fart sometimes – don't feel embarrassed!'

"Anyway, I finally get rid of the fucker, he saw the light, I was a hopeless case. He says to the old lady, 'If I were you I'd kick that young whelp out in the streets, let him find his own food and shelter. I've run into some impudent characters – but this one – ' And away he goes, out the door, leaving a trail of smoke. I didn't lose no time myself. This all happened about an hour ago. The first thing I done was duck into the old lady's room and pocket her grocery money, six bucks and some change, then I went upstairs and packed my things and got these fancy duds on and walked out. I didn't say a word, I just walked past her and out the door, not a thing, not so much as goodbye or kiss my arse. That's the last time she'll see me in that house."

"Where do you intend to go?" I asked him.

"Well, I can't get far on six bucks... How much have you got? Are you with me?"

"I don't have a black cent. Let me think..."

"You must be able to raise something."

"Maybe in a few days... I'd like to, all right, that's not the problem. But it's no good trying to get anywhere broke. Where are you heading for, anyway?"

"I was thinking Montreal, maybe – but not with only six bills. On the way over I came up with an idea. I got an aunt in Saint John and I figure she could put us up till we found work, then we could get a place of our own... Only I don't know if she'd want to take the two of us in. She's a stingy old cunt. I'll be lucky if she'll let me stay there... Look, I tell you what, I got to get moving, it gets dark early and if I'm gonna make it to Saint John I can't waste any time – it's easier, one guy thumbing, anyway... What I'll do is, go down there and stay with my aunt and find a job quick and get my room, then I'll write you right away, and by that time you should have some coin and you can join me. It'll be no sweat, the two of us getting work, all we have to do is try for a change, put out minds to it. We'll work for a couple of months, maybe a month or so and save every cent and then take off south where it's warm. I'm getting sick of all that snow and cold every winter, we'll boot it down to Mexico and lie around in the sun and drink tequila and fuck the senoritas. How's that sound?"

That's what we agreed on. I saw him to the door, told him again I had no money at the moment, nothing to lend him, not even a nickle — which was true — and said I'd see him in a week or whenever he got a place. The sooner the better.

Then I watched him hustle off down the street, stepping along with the fallen leaves flying in his wake, a young man to whom no obstacle would be too great...

I'd wait for his letter. It was Sully after all, so no point getting too carried away, expecting things that probably wouldn't happen.

PART TWO

IT WAS ONE WEEK to the day when I heard from him, a brief unpunctuated letter riddled with misspellings, the handwriting large and unpracticed like a grade schooler's. The letter was dated Friday but postmarked Monday. He'd found a job with a collection agency, he wrote, starting Monday at a salary of forty-five dollars a week. Also he'd borrowed enough money off his aunt to rent a room on Sydney Street — "She wouldnt of gave me it but she was glad to get rid of me the old whore..."

He was pretty sure I could get a job with the same company if I wanted — if not there were plenty of other places to try. "So don't wast time kid get down hear on the duoble if ralf comes to tell him theirs room for him hear to."

I was able to raise ten bucks by selling my record collection dirty cheap, about thirty LP's in all. It pained me to do it, it had taken me years to beg borrow and steal them, but that was my hole card, all I owned that was saleable. The record player itself I didn't try to sell. It was my late mother's and I wouldn't have felt right doing that. I think it belonged to my oldest sister anyway, by right of inheritance.

When the ten bucks in my pocket I packed my knapsack and left a brief note on the kitchen table for the old man, donned my pea jacket, took a last look around my room and then struck off down the road to Ralph's place, on the remote chance he might be interested in coming along.

§

Stepping into Ralph's dingy rooming house out of the brilliant fall sun was like entering a crypt. In the semi-darkness I felt my way up the stairs and over the warped hall floorboards and knocked on his door. Though I'd heard voices there was silence now. I beat on the door again. "Ralph!"

"Who is it?"

"It's me."

"Oh. Just a minute."

With its two windows Ralph's room should have been bright, but both blinds were drawn and it was just as gloomy almost as out in the hall. The Bishop was with him. Judging by the number of empty wine bottles scattered around he'd been there quite some time. Ralph locked the door behind me and sat on the side of the bed. His eyes were moist and distant looking. He was obviously drunk.

"Welcome to the party," said Ralph.

"What's going on?"

"The Bishop's hiding out."

The Bishop was sitting on the only chair, round, moon-faced, his back stiff and his hands resting palms down on his thighs. There was an open quart of Napoleon Canadian sherry on the chest of drawers beside him. They were drinking the good stuff; Napoleon cost a dime more than Hermit or Challenge or the other staples.

"We thought you were the law," said Ralph. "Did you bring anything to drink?... We've got something here somewhere. Give the man a drink, your highness..."

The Bishop stirred; he hadn't shown any indication he'd seen me come in. He made a sign of the cross with his hand over the bottle and mumbled some Latin.

"We don't drink unblessed wine," said Ralph. "That's why we're so holy..." He laughed. "We're some holy all right... the only thing holy about me is my drawers."

I took a swig and said, "I'm in a hurry, I'm heading for Saint John, Ralph. What's this about hiding out?"

"Saint John? What are you going there for? What's all this about everyone going to Saint John? That's where Sully is. I saw him before he left. He wanted me to go with him... Saint John... that's a hell of a place to go. What've they got that we don't have? Why not go to New York?"

"Maybe we will – later on."

"I guess we better go with you.. What do you think, Bishop, you want to go to Saint John?"

"*Miserere nostri, Domine.* Yes, certainly, my son."

"It's no good thumbing with three," I said, "nobody'll stop for three guys–"

"We'll have to wait till dark before leaving," Ralph said. "What time's the bus leave?"

"I'm not taking any bus," I said. "I can't waste money on buses. I'm hitchhiking."

"We can't leave before dark."

"Why's that? You can't get a drive at night."

"The Bishop's a wanted man, the law's on his trail. And I'm an accessory, harbouring a fugitive. I think I should get out of town, I think the both of us better get out and never come back..."

"What's he done, steal wine from the nuns again?"

"That's one thing, but it's not the main thing. Six quarts of Napoleon he had — yesterday — a half dozen. He didn't tell me till this morning, where he got the money to buy all that wine... Holy sufferin'... Tell him where you got the money."

"*Dominus vobiscum*..." The Bishop tipped the bottle and put it down, glowing.

"He broke into the offerings box," said Ralph. "That's getting pretty bad."

"Oh."

"He's been hiding here ever since. I should've got rid of him... But after the wine was gone he still had some money left, so I used it to buy a few more bottles."

"Do they know it's him?"

"I don't know what they know. But they must know he's the one took the two gallons from the convent... they might figure who does that kind of thing."

"Hmm. Well, I'll be seeing you, Ralph."

"Maybe they don't know, they mightn't have any proof. Where are you off to? What's your rush. We have to talk this over if we're going travelling."

"But it's no good, three together – and in broad daylight, with the Bishop – it'll look like he's running away."

"So you don't want to take him, is that it?"

"It's not that..."

"If he can't go, I don't go. You hear that? If he can't go, I don't go. I stick with my friends, I don't leave my friends behind."

"There's another thing – Sully only has a single room, he couldn't put three people up. It'll be crowded as it is."

"Why couldn't he? There's three of us here and there's space for one more. His room can't be smaller than this. Let's get going."

"I don't know, Ralph."

"The Bishop's not good enough for you, is that it?"

"It's not that, Ralph –"

"If he wants to come, he can come. Do you want to come, your excellency?"

"Oh yes. Certainly, Ralph."

"There. How much money do we have? Money. We need money if we're going to go travelling the world. How much do I have... let me see." He dug into his pocket and held out his hand. "Yes, well, at least money is no obstacle. Eight cents. Now what else do we need. Bishop, how much do you have?"

"Um..." The Bishop came up empty. "You wouldn't care to buy a chalice, would you?" he said to me.

"No, thanks."

"The hell with it," said Ralph. "We got no goddamn money, we can't go anywhere. We couldn't get halfway to Clifton let alone Saint John." He looked away, sinking into himself. "I don't want to go to Saint John anyway... What's there in that town for me? I don't need Saint John, I can't go running around like a hobo. I'm a musician... A musician like me couldn't make anything in a two-bit town like Saint John... Piss on it..."

He looked as though he didn't intend to say anything further, so I said, "Well, I have to get going."

"Going? Where're you going?"

"It gets dark early, I've got a lot of road to cover. I probably won't make it all the way today as it is."

"I always thought you were my friend."

"What's that got to do with anything?"

"I used to think... you were my *friend*." When he said "friend" his lips formed an ugly curl.

"I am. I dropped in to see if you wanted to come with me, but you don't."

"Who said I don't? I can't. Can you lend me some money?"

"I don't have very much... what for?"

"So the Bishop and I can take the bus down."

"I don't have enough for that – not nearly enough–"

"Well, shit on it, if you don't want my friends along–"

"Look, Ralph, it's not that –"

"Aw – I got no friends, what am I talking about, friends. I got no friends... not in this town...

they all figure I'm a pushover. They don't think I can fight."

"Fight?"

"Yeah, fight. That's what I said. But they'll find out... anyone tries to push me around... they'll learn. I'm a *karate* expert... Did you know that?"

"No."

He got to his feet, but none too steadily, and made a punch at the wall, his fist stopping about six inches short of it. "There. See that?" He did it again and again, grunting each time. "Unh! Unh! Unh!"

"Watch you don't hit your hand."

"I won't hit my hand. I know what I'm doing. Anyone tries to tangle with me they're in trouble... *real* trouble." He had a nasty hateful look on his face. "And I'm taking a course... a *special* course... in fighting... You know what kind of fighting?... *dirty* fighting... *dirty... fighting...* I'm studying *dirty fighting...* do you hear that? Nobody wants to mess around with *this* guy."

"You're getting awful fierce, Ralph."

"I'm fierce all right. I can beat — I can take on *anyone.* Anyone in this town. I used to think I had some friends around here... Are you still my friend? We used to be friends once upon a time."

"Sure, we're friends. What's the trouble, anyway?"

"Aw, I don't know. I'm just disgusted. I'm getting nowhere. I don't know whether I'm coming or going." He calmed down, his expression softened, his fighting visage slipped away as suddenly as it had appeared. "Where's the wine anyway?" He got his hands on it and took a very thorough drink, almost draining the bottle, leaving barely a mouthful in the bottom. "We have to get another one of these."

The Bishop reached over and took the bottle from him and finished it off. "Amen," he said.

I was standing by the door and now I unlocked it. "I can't hang around any longer, Ralph. You and the Bishop can come along later, if you want. Take a bus, hitchhike after dark, whatever you like. Try to get hold of some money."

"What's the address down there?"

I wrote it on a matchcard for him and he put it in his pocket.

"Okay, I might be down, soon as I get the money," he said.

"Yes. When, ah... the heat's off," said the Bishop.

"We're all still good friends. Right?" said Ralph.

"Right. So I'll see you when you come down."

My next stop was the Liquor Store where I picked up a bottle of Hermit and then I walked to a place on the road to Clifton known as "the corner" where everyone hitchhiked, though there was no corner there but just a stretch of road near the edge of town.

§

Miller, he said his name was. I'd been standing for more than an hour under a streetlight on the outskirts of Fredericton when he came sauntering out of the shadows and halted beside me. "No luck, eh?" he said.

"No. It's kind of late." I waited for him to move on, but he stayed where he was; the headlights of a car approached and he jerked out his thumb and the car drove on past.

"Where you headed for?" he wanted to know. I told him Saint John and he said, "Good, that's where I'm going. We'll thumb together. It'll give us a better chance."

"You think so?" I looked at him closely. As far as I could tell I'd never set eyes on him before. He was a rough surly-faced fellow somewhere around my own age. "I don't know, I think it's easier for one guy alone."

"No sir. You're wrong there." He glared at me as though I'd grossly insulted him, and he wasn't going to stand for it. "If we work separate we'll need to get twice as many drives. We're better off sticking together. I know all about hitchhiking. I been all over New Brunswick, plenty of times."

"Well, I know something about it myself."

"I'm always on the road. I been all over New Brunswick."

"I thumbed to Toronto – just this summer–"

"So did I. Plenty of times. We'll get a ride, don't you worry. I know what I'm doing."

Another car came along and drove on by and we stood without speaking for a while. Finally I said, "I think we'd be better off in separate places."

"We'll stick together. That's the best way."

"I'm not so sure... especially after dark. I think I'd rather try by myself."

"We'll get a ride. You just watch."

After a few more cars sped past us, I decided I had to do something; it was quite late even now, almost nine o'clock, and my hopes of reaching Saint John on my own were dim enough, without this guy by my side.

While I didn't like the idea of having him in front of me getting first crack at the drives – or scaring them off altogether – it looked as though I was going to have to give up my place; he obviously wasn't going to move on, and I could see that nothing would be gained by arguing with him about it.

"I'll tell you what," I said. "You can have this spot and I'll move along a ways. I think that'll give us both a better chance. Maybe I'll have more luck up ahead."

"Why do that? There's nothing wrong with where we are."

"No, but you can stay here. I don't mind. Good luck."

I started off down the road, but I didn't get far before I heard him coming along behind me. He caught up and said, "I'll go with you, there's probably a better place further along."

I stopped at the next streetlight. I didn't know how I was going to get rid of him.

In a few minutes a station wagon came along and Miller stuck his thumb out at arm's length, jerking it up and down vigorously, like telling the driver to shove it – which was another reason I wasn't too eager for his company; nobody was going to stop with him gesturing like that.

"The next one'll pick us up," he said.

"Sure. Look, it's kind of late for hitchhiking. I think I'll call it quits and head back for Fredericton."

"Where'll you go?"

"Maybe the jail."

"Yeah, we could always go there. They'll put us up."

"Or maybe I'll just walk around all night."

"Might as well stay here then, as do that. Somebody's going to give us a lift. You watch."

A few more cars went by and he gave them the thumb, jabbing it violently at the air. All of a sudden he turned away from the road and began staring at me intently, scrutinizing me. " I could tell you something," he said, "but you wouldn't listen."

"What's that?"

"Nobody ever listens. They say they do, but they don't. I can't be bothered telling them anymore. It's too late anyway, they'll find out soon enough."

Another car came towards us. He didn't seem to notice it, he was still gazing at me. Automatically I put my thumb out – and immediately regretted it; it struck me that I didn't want the car to stop, not until I'd lost this guy Miller. But I left my thumb out anyway – because it was there, from force of habit – thinking the car would pass us by in any event. Yes, it went on by, and then pulled over and stopped.

"I told you," Miller said, dragging me along by the arm. When we reached the car he held the door open for me to get in first.

"How far are you going?" I asked the driver. He was an elderly man in a plaid work jacket.

"Get in, get in," said Miller impatiently. He shoved me through the door.

"Are you going all the way to Saint John?" I said.

Miller closed the door after us. The car started away.

"I said — are you going all the way to Saint John?"

The man turned his head slowly towards me, then back to the road.

"Saint John? Why, is that where you're headed?"

"Yes. Are you going there?"

"What would I be going to Saint John for?"

"You're not going that far?"

"Well, not quite. But I'll help you out some. I'll get you closer than you are now."

"If you're not going to Saint John—"

"How far are you going?" asked Miller.

"Well, do you know where Oromocto is?"

"Yeah."

"I'm not going there, but it's near there. It's a little beyond that. It's not far from a place called Geary. Ever hear of it?"

"I have," said Miller.

"That's no good, I'm trying to get to Saint John," I said.

"It's all right, I know the place," said Miller. "We'll be able to hitch a ride from there easy."

"But..." Indecision. I hesitated — I could ask the man to stop, to let me off — but we were moving along at a steady clip and were already some distance out of Fredericton; and Miller would likely get off too, the way he was leeching onto me; I'd still be stuck with him. I was a little worried about the guy, he didn't seem to have all his marbles. In any case I couldn't make up my mind in time, and so we kept driving on.

At least we were going in the right direction, on the road to Saint John.

§

"This is as far as I'm going, boys. The best I can do for you. I turn off here."

We climbed out and the car turned up a side road and in a minute its tail lights disappeared and its engine gradually died away. We stood in the cold still darkness. There was just a faint glow in the sky where the moon was hidden by clouds but it was enough to see we were in the middle of nowhere, on a stretch of road between two unbroken walls of thick black forest. If there was a place called Geary around here it wasn't making itself too conspicuous.

"Now look where we are. For Christsake..." I felt quite dejected – and apprehensive.

"Let's go," said Miller. "We better not hang around here."

"Go where? Where's there to go?"

I stayed put. If he wanted to take a stroll, fine; the further he got the better. I heard his voice down the road. "Follow me. If you stay here you're done for."

"What do you mean?"

"You'll find out. I been in this part of the woods before. Hurry up, they'll be coming soon."

"Who?"

"You'll find out. Listen."

I listened – I couldn't say that I heard anything – but on the other hand – I caught up to Miller.

"What do you mean? Who's back there?"

"Shh! Listen." We listened. "Did you hear that? I think they're following us."

"Who? What're you talking about?"

"I can't tell you now. I knew they were coming. Nobody would listen and now it's too late. They can't blame me."

We set off down the highway at a rapid pace. After some minutes I said, "Where are we going? We can't walk all the way to Saint John."

"No. We're going to Hartland."

"Hartland?"

"Hartland. We can get work there picking potatoes. I know the farmers, I can get us on."

"Hartland's not this way — it's on the other side of Fredericton."

"You're wrong, it's up ahead. I know this road. I've been over it hundreds of times."

"I don't want to pick potatoes—"

"We can make good money at it."

"The season's all over anyway, it's almost winter—"

"Look, don't try and tell me about picking potatoes. I know all about picking potatoes. We'll be working tomorrow."

"Well, it won't be in Hartland, not going in this direction. I don't care what you say."

He stopped and squared himself in front of me. "I told you it's up ahead. Didn't you hear me? Are you dumb or something?"

"Take it easy — okay, it's this way, whatever you say."

We continued on. I glanced repeatedly over my shoulder and at length saw the lights of a car coming. I put my thumb out.

"Don't bother," said Miller. "It won't stop. Wait — it might be them — be careful—"

I kept my thumb out and the lights flared in my face and were gone as the car rushed past.

"You better be careful. You don't know who that might've been. If they'd stopped—"

"What? Who're you talking about?"

"Don't say I didn't warn you."

We resumed walking, Miller ahead, myself trailing behind. Little by little my steps lagged, I let myself fall gradually further behind him, hitting my heels hard on the pavement so he'd think I was closer to him than I was, until before long I could just barely make out his dark form ahead. I marked time on the road, and then I turned and started walking the other way.

"Hey! Where are you?" he hollered.

I halted. I heard him coming my way. I turned and began walking towards him. "What is it?" I said.

"What're you doing? Why don't you keep up with me?"

"You're going too fast. I'm getting tired."

"Don't fall so far behind. It's dangerous."

We started off again, and again I gradually slipped further and further behind, slowing and shortening my stride a little each step. I walked softly so he couldn't hear my footsteps, to see what would happen. Perhaps his mind would get so engrossed in Hartland and potatoes and the mysterious whoever-they-were that he'd forget about me altogether. I came to a complete stop. By the sound of his steps he seemed quite far ahead. I was about to turn and run like hell when he shouted, "Hurry up! What's keeping you? Do I have to go back and drag you?" He didn't seem that far away, after all.

"I'm coming! I'm right behind you!"

I trotted up to him and said, "My sock fell down in my boot, I had to stop and fix it."

"You want to stick close, boy. You know what they'll do if they catch you."

"Right."

A few paces onward he said, slowly, "I'm beginning to wonder about you."

"What do you mean?" I said.

"How do I know you're not one of them yourself?... That's what I'm wondering about. You know, I think you are. I think you're trying to trap me."

"No, I'm not. I don't even know who you're talking about."

"You don't, eh?"

"No."

"If I ever thought – If I thought for a minute you were one of them–"

"I'm not – whoever they are – believe me–"

"You better be telling the truth, or you're in big trouble, my friend. You won't be the first one I caught... That better be the truth."

"It is. Honest to God."

"Okay. I'll take your word. I believe you. But you want to stick close to me. That's the only way you'll be safe. They're afraid of me, they know what I'll do. I'm the only one they're afraid of. I've known about them for a long time. But try and tell anyone..."

He gripped my arm. "There's a light. See?"

"What is it?"

"I don't know. It's a house. Good."

"Why good?"

"We'll stay there for the night. We can go to Hartland tomorrow."

We walked closer and I was able to make out the silhouette of a building set back from the road, with a light in one of the downstairs windows. Behind the house rose the larger shape of a barn.

"How can we stay there? I don't think I want to."

"In the barn. We'll sleep in the barn. I've done that plenty of times."

"They probably won't let us."

"They won't know. Just be quiet. The only danger is – we can't be sure – who they are – it might be a trap–"

"Well, let's keep going."

"No. It's a good place to sleep. I'll find out if it's safe – I'll check first. Come on, follow me."

"Jeez, I don't know–"

"Don't make any noise."

"Look, you understand this kind of thing, you go ahead by yourself and check first. I'm liable to give us away. I'll come behind you, I'll stick just a bit behind and you signal when it's all right."

"Don't get too far behind me."

"No, I'm with you."

Crouched low and moving stealthily he started for the house. I followed a few steps into the yard and stopped. For a minute I lost him in the shadows and then he reappeared on the far side of a woodpile, partially in the light from the window. He darted from the woodpile to the side of the house and again I lost him. At first I walked backwards, getting out onto the road again, then I moved off on my toes in the direction we'd come from, looking back all the time at the house. Miller reappeared in the light – my last sight of him was his head outlined against the lower part of the window, he was squatting there peering in. I reached the end of a field and with trees between me and the house I tore off at a dead run, racing full tilt down the highway as fast as my legs could carry me. When I had to slow to a walk my heart was pounding in my ears and I couldn't hear if he was coming or not. He might still be back there, gesturing for me, calling in a whisper, searching around the yard... or he might right this minute be in hot pursuit; convinced now that I was one of "them" and he had to catch me and deal with me, as he'd dealt with the others...

§

The Volkswagen almost ran me down, swerving as it braked with a jolting suddenness. I climbed in, breathing relief, hardly able to believe my luck – the first car that happened along – Miller wouldn't catch me now –

It was going in the direction of Fredericton, back the way I'd come, but I didn't care, I was hitchhiking both sides of the road, anything to get out of there.

By the faint light of the dash I saw that the driver was a young fellow, no more than eighteen. The tie he was wearing was tugged loose, hanging like a limp kerchief around his neck; his hair was rumpled; every few minutes he lifted a quart of beer from between his legs and guzzled a drink.

He was drunk as a nit, absolutely pissed—

"Drinka beer?" He passed the bottle across to me and the motion caused the car to veer sharply. He righted it, chuckling to himself.

I downed as much of the quart as I could in one drink.

"Lots more... wanna bottle?"

He reached over the back of the seat.

"No – watch it!" We were flying along about eighty down the wrong side of the road.

"No? Don' wanna quarta beer?"

"You're on the wrong side of the road."

"Oh... Yeah, guess I am." He laughed. The car rocked over to the other lane and back again and over again before straightening out. Lights were coming our way. It looked to me we were headed straight at them.

"Hey, watch it, be careful," I said.

"Wassa matter? You think I can't drive or something?"

We almost put the oncoming car in the ditch, and he said, "No sweat, my frien', no sweat. I know how to handle this sonvabitch, drove 'er all the way from Halifax... drank lotsa beer too." He laughed stupidly and raised the bottle and drained what I'd left, his head thrown back, eyelids closed. The car weaved from side to side. He belched, rolled down the window and tossed the empty out on the highway. My eyes were glued to the road; I was tense as a board, suctioned to the seat, one hand gripping the handle on the dash.

"Gotta have nuther beer," he said. "Gotta open nuther quart."

"We're almost to Fredericton — no point in opening one now—"

"Awmost Fred'ton... how far we gotta go?"

"Only a couple of miles."

"Couple miles..." He laughed. "Don't know where I am. Think I'm gettin' little tight."

"Yeah, I think so."

"But I can drive, can still drive... don' worry, my frien', I can handle 'er awright..."

The miles that went by were agonizing; I'd scarcely drawn a breath since I got in the car. I was gambling we'd get within walking distance of Fredericton and then I'd get out and foot it the rest of the way. We were doing close to eighty and miraculously managing to keep between the ditches... but how long could that keep up? After about fifteen hair-raising minutes I was saying to myself, "One more mile, just one more mile will do it... I'll tell him to stop... while I'm still alive..." and a mile would go by and we hadn't cracked up, and we were that much closer to Fredericton... but my nerves couldn't take much more. Another mile... I'll give him another mile... it's still a long hike... I glanced over at him and his head was nodding. It dropped, then snapped up. He kept it upright for a while but it rolled around like it was on a ball bearing. It dropped again, jerked up.

"For christsake, don't fall asleep."

"Won' fall asleep..."

"Slow down. I get out here—"

"Wha's that?..."

"I said stop." There was a bend up ahead, a downward slope in the road and a sweeping turn at the foot of it. I had a sick feeling in the pit of my stomach. The guy was still nodding and he hadn't slowed.

"Get out here... nothin' here... where 'bouts?"

We were still driving at the bend as if the road continued straight through the trees. "Slow down!" His head turned and he looked at me vaguely. At the last second my hand reacted on its own, it caught the wheel and I leaned on it and we hit the gravel and went swerving and fishtailing around the turn, coming within a whisker of rolling over into the ditch.

"You moron!"

He gave me a foolish laugh. "Wassa matter?"

"Pull over. I'm getting out. If I hadn't grabbed that wheel–"

"Nothin' to worry about, I was watchin'... gonna make the turn..."

"Yeah, I could see that."

"Awfa nervous guy."

When he let me out I was shaking like a leaf. I took a long snort of wine, pointed myself towards Fredericton, and started walking.

For the next two hours I zigzagged the highway, thumbing both sides again, whichever way the cars happened to be travelling, catching their cold wakes in my face. The temperature had taken a sudden drop, it was below freezing by the feel of it. There wasn't much traffic. I thought as I walked of Sully in his warm room, wrapped in his blankets, snoozing away peacefully. Plodding along, dragging my feet. I was in sight of the Princess Margaret Bridge and then my luck changed. One of those rare things – unheard of – a *Cadillac* pulled over! The front window rolled down and the man in the passenger seat gave me a brief unfriendly glance but said nothing. He was in his fifties, beefy and jowly-faced, with a black felt hat on his head and a big cigar in his mouth.

It was the driver who spoke. "Where you headed for?" I leaned down to look in at him, by the light of the dash. He was a younger man, not more than twenty, wearing a leather jacket with the collar turned up.

"Saint John," I said.

"Well, we're going to Grand Bay. That's about ten miles from Saint John. If it's any help to you jump in."

"That'll do fine." It wasn't all the way but it was close enough. I'd leapfrog over Miller, get warmed up in the car, put time as well as distance behind me and when I got there I could walk until daylight; walk the whole way in, if I had to.

I got in the back and shut the door and settled myself down in the soft leather seat, stretched my legs out full length and let the warmth envelop me. It was a delicious feeling. The Cadillac rolled along quietly and for a short time nobody said anything. Then the older man piped up, "Earl, we shouldn't pick up strangers like that." His voice was whiney. "You never know who they are. We don't know who this guy is."

"What difference does it make?" The one called Earl spoke softly. "He doesn't know who we are either."

"We should be staying overnight in Fredericton anyway. It's too late to be driving on. We should get a motel. Earl? Why don't we stop and get a motel. There's still time, there's one not far ahead. Earl?"

"It won't take long to get there."

"Earl, it's late. You must be tired after driving all this way."

"I'm not tired."

"Why don't we stop? What do you say? Why not. Eh, Earl? We can let this guy off, he can always get another ride."

But Earl kept driving on.

"Look, there's the motel ahead." A neon light was flashing *Pine Grove Motel*, and other lights announced *shower*, *TV*, *restaurant*, and *vacancy*.

"Earl, it says vacancy."

We drove on past the motel.

"Dammit, Earl, you should've stopped, now we've got to drive all the way. Why don't we go back?"

Earl ignored him.

"Don't be sore at me, Earl. You're not sore at me, are you? Earl? Christ, I just thought it'd be wiser if we got some rest and went on in the morning..."

We drove in silence for some time and the warmth and motion began putting me to sleep. I rubbed my eyes, propped the lids up with my fingers, gave my head a couple of shakes.

"Getting enough heat back there?" said Earl.

"What? Oh — yeah, it's just great."

"It's a cold night to be out on the road."

"You're right."

"I know what it's like... It's too bad we're not going all the way to Saint John."

"That's okay. I'll manage."

A few minutes later he said, "I think we should take him all the way in."

"Earl! Earl, we can't do that, we're not going that far, it's late, we have to get to bed – Aw, Earl–"

"I think we should." He shrugged. "But it's your car."

"For Christsake, Earl. We don't know this guy. You don't want to drive all the way into the city... Earl?"

§

An hour later I watched the Cadillac drive off, the fat old guy scowling and chewing on his cigar. I was standing in front of a darkened building on Sydney Street in Saint John. It was the address Sully had given me in his letter, and on the door was a sign saying *Rooms*.

§

It was a better class of building than I expected, had a locked inner door and buzzers to the rooms. There was no answer when I rang number six. I pressed the button again and again, listening. Not a sound. I stepped outside and rechecked the house number. It was right – the one Sully had given me, anyway. At the nearest corner a traffic light hummed and clicked, changing color for the empty street. Everything else still, silent, closed-up and in darkness.

It was too late in the night to rouse the superintendent, assuming there was one in the building. There wasn't much I could do. I went back to the vestibule where it was slightly less frigid than the outdoors and settled myself down on the floor and rolled a smoke and got the wine bottle out of my pack.

Sometime later I dozed off – but only for a few minutes – it was too cold to sleep, I awoke shivering, my breath steaming.

I went out and walked up and down the street a while – then came back and smoked and drank the last of the wine. I fell into a fitful sleep. When I awoke it was still dark and I was frozen stiff.

It wasn't until eight o'clock – well after daylight – that I heard signs of life within, someone coming down the stairs. I got stiffly to my feet and opened the outer door as though I'd just stepped in.

"Morning," I said. A man in a construction helmet with a lunch pail under his arm walked past, nodding briefly. I caught the inner door before it swung to and went inside.

Room number eight was on the second floor. I rapped on the door. No answer. I knocked harder.

"Open up, Sully! Open up! Is you in there, Sully?" But I wasn't in the mood for Cookie jokes. I tried the knob and found the door wasn't locked. I opened it an inch, not knowing what to expect. Sully dead in his bed, a knife sticking out of his back? I'd had plenty of time during the night to entertain all sorts of wild possibilities. I shoved the door open further and stuck my head in, prepared for anything. But there was no one there, not a soul – just a lot of rubbish – beer and wine empties, cigarette butts, pizza cartons, shrivelled-up french fries, bread crusts, paper plates, plastic forks... The air reeked, stale and fumid. The bed was unmade, the sheets filthy. It looked like

Sully's room all right, wherever he was now — though I wondered if even he could have left such a mess, all by himself. I checked the closet and chest of drawers. They were empty, no coat, no suitcase, no pair of socks, no comb, nothing to identify the missing occupant but a lot of garbage, and anyone could have left that behind.

§

The janitor's sleeves were rolled to his biceps and his arms were swathed in tattoos, not an inch of natural skin showing above the wrists. I found him in his basement room at the foot of a steep stairway.

"You a friend of his?" He squinted at me.

"Uh, not exactly. I'm just supposed to give him a message."

"Well, I can't help you. He was here till last night and then him and his buddies fucked off — the little cunt. If I get my hands on him... Come here, I want to show you something. Come upstairs."

He turned me around by the elbow and I followed him upstairs to Sully's room and he flung open the door. "Take a look at that. What do you think of that?"

"Jeez." I shook my head in awe. "Looks like a tornado hit it."

"A tornado? No fuckin' tornado ever left a mess that bad. They were in here drinking and making a helluva racket, all day yesterday and the night before, in and out and in and out. I had to come up a couple of times and shut them up. The last time they went out I checked the room and this is how I found it. Packed his stuff and fucked off, leaving the room like a goddamn garbage dump. Anyone'd leave a place in this kinda shape—"

"Any idea where he went? I don't suppose you'd know..."

"I don't know and I don't care. But if I run across him again he'll remember it, I'll pound the shit out of him. I'm the one's got to clean up after him and I don't fuckin' like it. You think I got nothing else to do around here? Eh?"

§

I had no luck on my first call. "No," the voice said, "no one by that name works here."

I hung up and signalled the waiter. He left his coffee and morning paper and tapped a beer and brought it to my table. At that hour of the morning the tavern was just waking up, no more than half a dozen customers. After a mouthful of beer I tried another collection agency.

"Sullivan?" The voice was hoarse and aggressive. "Guy calls himself Rico Sullivan?"

"Rico? No... Wait, yeah, right, that'd be the one."

"What do you want with him?"

"I'm just trying to look him up. I got into town a few hours ago and I thought I'd get in touch."

"So you don't know where he is?"

"That's why I'm calling you. Someone told me he worked for a collection agency."

"You know him well?"

"No... no, not all that well."

"Hmm." There was a pause at the other end.

"Well, I'm looking for him too. You tried his place?"

"The janitor said he moved out last night. He doesn't know where he went."

"I tried his place a couple of times myself yesterday. Just missed him."

"He's working for you, is he?"

"He's *supposed* to be. Only I ain't seen him around since Monday. He showed up for his first day and talked me into advancing him half a week's pay — talked *me* into it. I give it to him and next morning not a sign of him. And he ain't in again today and I don't expect he will be either. The little bastard's run out. A two-bit little crook. He's got a lot of goddamn nerve trying to take me for twenty bucks. I'll run him down. Where do you think he is?"

"If I knew I wouldn't be calling you—"

"I'll find the little fucker. I'm the last one he should've tried swindling."

"He only worked the one day?"

"Yeah, I was breaking him in, wanted to give him an idea what the job's like. Maybe he just didn't have the guts for the work. A guy with his mouth, I thought he could handle it. What do you know about this bird anyway? What's your name? Between the two of us maybe we can find him."

"I doubt it. Thanks anyway — Goodbye."

"If you run into him tell him to get that money back to me, and quick — or I'll have him hauled up on a fraud charge — after I break his fuckin' neck—"

On the wharf at the foot of King Street I watched a pair of tugboats shepherding a ship through the fog, their horns sounding, the boats appearing and disappearing like spirits. The tide was high, the waves rolling in in great swells almost to the top of the wharf. A megaphoned voice came out of the fog. "Do you have a cable there?" And a minute later, "There doesn't seem to be a cable."

An old man came up to where I was standing – gesturing, muttering to himself. "They're moving her to a different berth," he observed.

"Can't see much today."

"No, it's the fog." He watched a moment, then turned and vanished the way he'd come. In front of me a seagull skimmed over the surface alighting delicately on the water, tucking in its wings, rising and falling with the swell, the water oily, full of refuse. At the next wharf the spectre of a large ship with a Korean flag was taking on cargo – winches whining, rattling – phantom longshoremen moving about the deck –

I'd been all over the city, poking my nose into every tavern, searching for Sully. I had the worst suspicions and can't say I expected to find him. I'd even gone over to the West End, the other side of the harbour, looking for taverns there, up and down dismal streets of clapboard tenements, flat-roofed, misshapen, sagging to the right and left, painted brown and dark green. Chalk scrawls on the walls – "S.C. is a little hore looking for tale" – "Debbie Sucks Cocks" – Broken toys in the weeds, runny-nosed kids.

The fog was thicker over there, carrying a stench from the mill in that end, as much smog as fog. There were quite a few churches, their stone walls coated with soot, but no taverns that I could find. It was too far to walk back so I splurged on a bus; I was pretty sure I was screwed anyway, I'd never make it on my own with what I had, so I might as well spend it. Blow the works.

There was one thing I could ascertain anyway. I found a phone booth and dropped a dime in the slot and got the long distance operator. I could check this much for free.

"I want to make a collect call to Bannonbridge. Yes, collect. Mister Percy Sullivan Junior."

After a minute the operator talking... "A collect call for Mr. Percy Sullivan Junior from..."

It was Sully's old lady on the phone. When she heard who was calling she said, "No, he certainly won't accept the charges."

So there it was —

"He's not here now anyway," she said.

I broke in — "You mean he didn't come back after all — from Saint John—"

"So that's where he was, was it? He came back — *early* this morning."

"Oh." Dead drunk no doubt — He was probably this very minute sleeping it off — She didn't want to say that —

The lousy rotten bastard —

§

Visions of Sully hanging by his thumbs, dangling, twisting, his eyes bulging at the sight of the knife. He begs, whines like a puppy. A swipe of the knife and his danglers fly through the air and out the window...

The Imperial Tavern is a long narrow room that broadens at the rear, the walls lined with framed photographs and paintings of Saint John in former days: sailing ships, horses and carriages, rugby teams, soldiers on parade, a visiting Royal Family, historical sites. There's a large fireplace and panelled wainscoting and a huge fat waiter. It's quite the establishment. Everyone seems to know everyone else. Sailors, longshoremen, pensioners, derelicts... There's no air-conditioning and everyone's got a cigarette butt in his mouth, a veil of smoke swirling about the tables.

Two South Korean seamen are ashore for a night's drinking, sitting with some local drunks. They're off the ship I saw loading earlier. One of them sings "La Paloma" and for an encore does "Great Balls of Fire". He's got a terrible voice, and doesn't know English, he's memorized the sounds of the words to the songs, but the drunks at the table clap and holler encouragement. The other Korean hardly opens his mouth. The drunk beside him is doing his best to surmount the language barrier, bridge the cultural gap, if you will. "I've heard of your Prime Minister, or whatever you call him," he says. "I know who that is. What's his name – Jesus, it's on the tip of me tongue – Chow Un Lie? That's it, ain't it? Chow Un Lie?"

The quiet Korean is trying to ignore him.

"That's right, ain't it? You know, he's a big guy over in your country. I'm trying to think of his name – Chow Un Lee – Chow Un Lie – C'mon, you must know him."

The Korean leans away, shaking his head.

"Don't get me wrong, I'm not trying to be funny. But ain't that the guy, over there where you come from?"

The Korean offers him a cigarette, then holds the package for the others, all the drunks taking one. "I mean, what's that name, what's he called? Chow Un Lie? Ching Chang Chong? Who Flung Dung? One Hung Low?... You understand any of this?"

A man in work clothes is standing over an older man who's sitting nearby drinking alone. "You must know me," the younger one says. "You know *me*."

"I don't know you." The old guy puts his glass to his mouth. He doesn't want to be bothered by strangers.

"But you must."

"Naw, I never seen you before."

"I married your daughter."

"Yeah?" The old guy looks closer at him. "Yeah, I think I recognize you now. I got a lot of daughters. Sit down and have a beer."

I'm half-listening to a couple of old codgers sitting off to my left. "Will you stand me a beer, sir?" The one who speaks is wearing a threadbare corduroy jacket and half a pair of glasses — for his right eye — the other half broken off at the bridge —

"I can't," the other says. "The waiter won't serve you. He says you've had too much."

"Oh well." A pause. "You're okay, sir."

"Thank you. You're okay yourself."

"I'd love to get back to the old country." He's got a Scottish accent.

"Don't start picking your nose, sir."

The Scotchman takes out his handkerchief. "I have to pick something. I don't know how to pick pockets."

"Shake hands, sir. You're okay."

Drinking my beer, smoking, picturing Sully draped over a trestle, his wrists tied to his ankles by barbed wire, a funnel sticking out of his backside. I'm holding a bucket of wet cement and begin pouring — "You always wanted to be a big guy, Sully," I'll say. "You'll be a heavyweight now!"

An effeminate-looking fellow is at a table with two longshoremen, one of them wearing a watchcap. They're trying to get him to buy more beer, but he doesn't want to. They pay for a round themselves, to get him going, prime him, but he still won't order more. He doesn't even drink the glass in front of him, maybe thinking they want to get him drunk, empty his wallet. After a while they give up. The one with the watchcap says to the other, "Let's go."

"Where're we going, boys?"

"*We're* going back to the Bosun's Chair — but you're not, they won't let you in." At the door he says, so the whole tavern can hear, "You were acting too queer. You *are* too queer!" And they leave.

"I know... I'm queer." He sits by himself, chin sunk on his chest. I hear him mutter, "I don't care... Not really." After a few minutes he gets up to go, his glass of beer untouched. "I've had enough," he mutters. Going out the door he pauses and says to no one in particular, to himself, "Goodnight, gentlemen."

I'm too slow — before I can move someone reaches over and takes the full glass of beer he left behind.

More conversation going on...

"You work in Fredericton? How do you like it there?"

"Well, you know what they say. Saint John's the arsehole of Canada, but Fredericton's sixty miles up..."

"You and you and you – the two of yez can go fuck yourself–"

"The old woman's fifty-two and I'm fifty-two and we still poke away every night!"

"I dunno... I go home for a piece of tail after work, but to be fuckin' honest about it I'd rather have a good shit any day – You can't beat a good shit–"

Sully's treachery playing over and over in my mind. Thinking what I'll do to him when I see him next, going over all the medieval tortures I've read about...

It's getting late and they're closing up. I don't seem to have any money left anyway. At least I've got a room to go to for the night, a three-dollar room, paid for in advance. And another pack of cigarettes and a half bottle of wine there, waiting for me.

When I awake there's a gray light coming in the window. I feel as if I've been clubbed over the head with a crowbar. It takes me a minute to recognize the rented room – I can't remember how I got there. My cells are trembling, the blood jitterbugging through my veins. I have to throw up. On my way to the sink, bent-over like a cripple, I look out the window. It's snowing – a freak early storm, the snow blowing wild like smoke up the back alley, gusting and dancing, clinging to the fire escape –

When I leave the sink I sit on a chair by the window, watching the snow, imagining what the highway is like, wondering where I'm going to get the strength. There's a drink left in the wine bottle — I reach for it, then think better of it. I'll want it more on the road home, have something in reserve, not that it'll help much. For a minute or two I'll feel better, until it wears off — then it'll be worse than ever.

PART THREE

"MAC, GIVE US EIGHT, will you." Sully took out his wallet and deliberately, like a card sharp, placed a couple of bills on the table. "The old man give me five bucks to put the storm windows on," he said, "so I subcontracted the job — I got Roger to do it for a quart of wine—"

MacPherson brought a tray of beers and set them around the table, two in front of each of us.

"Rodge nearly fell off the ladder a few times but he got the job done. Where you been, anyway? I was just telling Nick you must've joined the monks or something."

"We thought you might be still in Saint John," said Nick, with a screechy little cackle.

"What a hole," said Harris. "You won't catch me down there again."

Nick and Harris — and Dearborn too, he'd been with them — I already knew, the story was around — they'd gone down in Nick's car the day before I set out hitchhiking. Nick had had a drunken phone call from Sully on the weekend, from George's Tavern, inviting the boys to come visit. The fact they actually went was pure chance. On Monday while Nick was driving about Bannonbridge with Harris they'd come across

Dearborn and Dearborn happened to have his unemployment cheque and so they bought some booze and — it was all on impulse. It never occurred to them to see if I wanted to go along, they just took off.

"We knew you'd be at school anyway," said Nick. "You should've let us know you wanted to come."

They had a fine old time of it — and when they left Saint John to return home Sully was with them.

"Put yourself in my place," Sully said to me.

I wasn't going to clobber him, I'd had a week or so to cool off. He was a lot smaller than me anyway. But I hadn't so much as nodded to him yet — I was going to ignore him, forever. It wasn't my fault they'd all come over to my table.

"I didn't know what I was getting myself in for," Sully said. "A collection agency... When I went for the job I hadn't a clue what it was, what they collected — stamps, for all I knew. I got the job Friday and the guy says come in Monday and he'll show me the ropes. The boss's name was Ward, a big fat fucker with a scar on his face — like Al Capone — that's who he looked like — He tells me I'm supposed to collect bad debts, to run down people who try to get out of paying their bills — sort of like a private detective, he said. It sounds pretty good, only what it really means is I'm supposed to go into the slums and squeeze money out of a lot of starving bastards who don't have a pot to piss in. They'd buy a fridge on credit, then borrow from the finance companies to meet the payments, then sell the fridge to pay the finance companies — only they never catch up because of all the interest they have to pay, it just keeps growing. So they say the hell with it all. I was supposed to go after these hopeless cases and

make them shit nickels if I have to – sell their kids, put
the old lady out hustling the streets – I was supposed
to bug them so much they'd do anything to get me off
their backs – make them feel like shit, take them to
court, grab their furniture, garnishee their pay – We
couldn't do most of that because most of them weren't
working and they didn't own fuck-all. But the idea was
to hound them and scare them enough that they'd get
the cash somewhere even if they had to steal it – just
to get rid of us. That was the idea I got. A great
company to work for. I went out with Ward on
Monday afternoon on a sort of trial run so I could
watch him operate. We went to a couple of places and
I got the idea, and then he wants me to show him what
I can do... This is what I mean, see? It was this
crummy old place in the West End and he points out
the door and kind of hangs back himself so he can
keep an eye on how I do – that's what I figure,
anyway, why he stops inside the door at the foot of the
stairs and don't go any further. The place is crawling
with kids – they're all niggers, running around with
rags on, there must've been two dozen of them,
howling and screaming and fighting... I have to go up
the stairs to an apartment on the second floor and
there's more kids up there, the place stinks, garbage on
the stairs. It's a real rathole, they're hanging over the
railing yelling at me. I knock on the door. 'Yeah, what
is it?' The door opens and there's this great big black
fucker, about eight feet tall – he has to stoop to look
out at me, he fills the whole doorway, standing there
in his undershirt – 'Pardon me, sir – ahem! – sorry to
bother you, but... ahem...' 'What you lookin' for?' He's
got a voice, you know, coming from away down here,

in his stomach. When I tell him I'm from the collection agency he takes a step forward and says, 'You get the fuck outa here, white arse, before I throw you down that stairs.'

"'Yes, sir. Whatever you say.' And I don't waste no time — I start down — but there's Ward watching me, the boss — so I stop halfway down the stairs and turn around — I've got enough of a head start, I figure — 'Listen, mister,' I say — and go into the spiel Ward learned me, about all the trouble we'll give him — haul him into court — plague him to death — the longer he puts it off the more he'll pay — we'll never let him go, we'll leach onto him worse than Harris. All this time he's pawing the floor with his foot up there, ready to charge, and I'm set to run like hell — but I keep talking cause the boss's taking it all in — I'm talking through the side of my mouth like Ward does. Then I notice something funny, like it's raining — it's weird, eh, raining indoors — it's not even raining outside — I look up and right above me there's a kid with his pecker poked through the bannister pissing on me, on my fuckin' head! 'You little bastard — ' And then the big guy comes after me. "I warned you, white arse — ' He comes charging down the stairs and I bolt out of there right behind Ward who's beating it out the door ahead of me. He's a tough guy himself, but not like that nigger.

"So I was going to quit then and there, I seen enough of that job. Soon as we got to Ward's car I opened my mouth to tell him what he could do with it — but then I thought — I already put in most of a day and if I quit now he won't pay me. So I said instead that I kind of liked the work, had learned a lot just in one day watching a pro like himself at it. I was pretty sure all the customers weren't as bad as that black son of a whore, and even if they were I'd find a way to handle them. I said somebody had to get these deadbeats to pay their debts, right? If the fuckers were gonna borrow money who'd they think they were, not paying it back? It was a tough job, sure, it took balls, but someone had to do the tough jobs in life. I said I could've taken that big nigger – a knee in the nuts, a chop to the throat – nothing to it, he didn't faze me – but I didn't think we were supposed to rough up the clients. He said that was right – we were getting along the very best, me and Ward – so I edged the conversation around to my own money problem. I said I was tempted to borrow from the finance company myself, just to see me through the week, to my first pay. I'd had to send my last cent to my mother who was in the hospital – the old man was dead, I explained. What I was working around to was getting my salary for that one day – I was gonna pop that at him in a minute – it wasn't like he didn't owe it to me – But he's a good judge of character, see, he knows a reliable guy when he sees one. 'I never done this before,' he says, 'and I ain't likely to do it again, but if you're that short I'll advance you half a week's pay – but it's only this once, understand? And you better put in a good fuckin' week's work to earn it.' I had to take it – I couldn't very well say I wasn't coming back tomorrow. Anyway, I thought I might stick it out a few more days, do fuck-all and get fired. But then Nick and Harris and Dearborn arrived – and you know the rest. It's a good thing I never told Ward I was from Bannonbridge. I said I was from Toronto so he wouldn't think I was a small-town hick or something, and he'll never find me up there. But I had to get out of Saint John, right?"

"Tell him about the whorehouse," said Nick.

"Wait'll you hear this," said Sully.

"You quiff, Sully," Harris said." You're some nice guy – You promised you wouldn't tell no one."

"Harris wanted to get laid when he got to Saint John, so I went with him to show him the place–"

"Don't give us that," said Nick. "You were after your hide too. But you chickened out."

"Like hell. I don't have to pay for it, I ain't like Harris." Turning to me he said, "Some guy in George's was gabbing at me one night down there, buying me beer and talking about all the whores he'd fucked, and he told me about this place on Cobourg Street – That's how I knew where to take Harris. I just went along for the laugh, for Christsake."

Sully went into some detail about it, how they left Nick and Dearborn in the Parrtown Tavern and went up a steep hill and down the other side towards the railway tracks, strolling along Cobourg Street trying to look casual while Sully looked for the house; he had only a general description to go by.

"I don't see a red light or nothing," Harris said. "It must be some other street." He was having second thoughts already. "What do you think, Sully? We'll never find the place – We might as well go back–"

Sully told him to calm down. "What are you so nervous about? You'd think you never been in a whorehouse before."

"I ain't nervous – this ain't me first time –"

"Go 'way, Harris–"

"When I was in Montreal with the old man—"

"Yeah, sure."

"Sully — look." A woman was sitting in a window at sidewalk level looking out at them, the drapes pulled behind her to hide the light from the room. They stopped, uncertain. "What do you think?" whispered Harris.

"It looks like the place," said Sully.

"What'll we do?"

"Give her a wave."

"Hey — She waved back! Now what?"

"Ask her if we can come in."

"She's awful hard-looking."

"Go ahead."

"Jesus, I don't like the looks of her."

"What do you expect — Marilyn Monroe?"

"Maybe she's just the old one that runs the place. Go ask her."

"Ask her yourself."

"No, you, Sully."

"C'mon, Harris, you're the one wanted to come here."

"You did too."

"Don't just stand there, Harris. Do you want your tail or not?"

"Fuck..."

Harris went closer to the window and in a voice hardly above a whisper said, "Can we come in?" The woman looked out questioningly.

"She can't hear you."

"I said can we come in?" he hollered.

The woman pointed in the direction of the door and disappeared behind the drapes. In a minute they heard a lock click and the door opened. She ushered them in quickly and closed the door behind them. They followed her a few steps down a hallway and into a shabby sitting room where there were two other women — one in her early twenties and the other considerably older. The young girl didn't look up; she was sitting in a corner knitting. The two older women were obviously sisters, possibly even twins. They were both somewhere in their fifties. They were grotesquely fat, with enormous paunches and legs like tree stumps and heads like withered old pumpkins.

"Give the gentlemen a seat, Phyllis," said the one who'd shown them in.

Phyllis was sitting on a moth-eaten couch with a deep sag in the middle. She got to her feet with some effort and toting a quart of beer hobbled across the room and sat on the stool by the window. "What's new, boys?" she said.

"Nothing much," said Sully. "My friend here wants to get laid."

"Hold on a minute, now," said Harris. He hadn't got his bearings yet. The wheels in his head gave a few ponderous turns. His eyes shifted from the young girl to the two old women, trying to assess the situation. Having been nowhere near a whorehouse before he was afraid of looking like a fool — doing something stupid, saying the wrong thing. The two old ones and the young one had him confused.

"How much is it?" he stalled. "I ain't too jeezless rich, you know."

"It don't cost much, love. It's bargain night."

"Well, how much?"

"You've got five dollars, now, haven't you?"

The fat old woman grinned at him. The girl continued to knit, wrapped in her thoughts, ignoring all of them. She was not bad-looking, at least to Harris's eye – and certainly by contrast to the others. Five dollars – He had that all right – but –

"Well..." He didn't want to come right out and ask, to look ignorant and inexperienced – Or to commit himself without knowing what he was getting in for –

"You got five bucks," said Sully. "Dearborn lent you ten–"

"Yeah, but I spent some – and I have to pay it back–"

Sully laughed.

"What's so jeezless funny?"

"What's the problem, dear? You didn't expect to pay less, did you?"

"Yeah, Harris, what's wrong with you? It don't come no cheaper."

"That's right, dear. Rock bottom."

"He's shy," said Phyllis.

Harris reddened. "I ain't shy, goddammit. Okay, okay. I just – You got any beer here? Do you bootleg? I want a fuckin' beer, I'm thirsty."

"Sure. Get him a beer, Vera."

"Get me one while you're at it," said Sully.

The one called Vera waddled through an open doorway to the kitchen and returned with two quarts of Moosehead.

"How much's that?" said Harris.

"A dollar each."

"Get mine, Harris," said Sully. "I'll pay you later."

"A buck a quart. Jeez, it's only seventy-five cents where we come from."

"Well, here you can sit and drink in comfort. It's worth an extra quarter." She laughed, her flesh rolling and shaking, showing a mouth pink with toothless gums. Harris looked away. Surely to Jesus — It had to be the young one —

"You can finish your beer after," said Vera, when he'd taken a couple of mouthfuls from the bootle. "Who's it gonna be now?"

Harris was in a sweat. He couldn't stall any longer. He was about to take his courage in his hands and blurt out, "Her," indicating the girl, though he didn't know if she was a whore or what she was. Or if they'd laugh in his face and say, "Oh, it'll cost you ten for her (or fifteen — or twenty) — but you said you had only a few dollars — " When in fact he did have more, hidden away in the corner of his wallet — but it was too late now —

"What do you say... Me or her?" Vera nodded at the other old one.

Harris's heart sank into his shoes.

"Don't be so goddamn slow," said Sully. "What'd you come here for, anyway?"

"Yeah — yeah, sure — what about you — what about —" Stammering.

"Never mind me. You wanted to get fucked, didn't you? Well now's your chance. You're not scared, are you?"

Harris looked this way and that. He rose to his feet. In desperation he spluttered, "What about her? Don't she ride?" There was a silence.

The young girl never took her eyes from her knitting.

"Sorry, love. That's my sister's daughter."

"She's deaf and dumb, poor thing," said Vera.

"Come along, lover. We ain't got all night, you know."

Harris stood rooted to the spot, pale, his eyes wild—

"He can't make up his mind," said Sully. "It's a tough choice."

"Well, I'll make it up for him," said Phyllis. "Come on, dear, this way."

Harris looked helplessly at Sully who turned away, coughing into his hand. There was an open door off the room and a bed in it covered with a yellowish sheet. A straight-backed chair stood at the foot of the bed. The woman lumbered in ahead of him and Harris, glancing bitterly back at Sully, followed her, dragging his feet like a man going to the gallows, a pathetic sight.

"Your friend don't look too happy," said Vera, when the door swung shut.

Sully continued to cough into his hand, his body shaking, choking — trying to get hold of himself—

"What is it, dear?"

"I was just thinking of something — nothing — My friend there — It's his first time, he's not used to this—" Getting control of himself. "He's a cheap bastard, too. It kills him to spend that five bucks—"

"How about you, love?"

"Me?"

"Don't you want to get yours, too?"

"No, no – I mean, thanks anyway – I wouldn't mind, but I don't have the scratch – I forgot my wallet—"

"Oh, you must have five dollars."

"Not on me, I don't."

"Ask your friend, he'll lend it to you."

"Him? Not a chance."

"I'm sure he would. Ask him anyway."

"Naw, I wouldn't waste my breath. He's tighter than a crab's cunt, that guy."

"You could pay him back. When he comes out, ask him–"

"He don't have it, anyway. All he had was about eight bucks and he paid two for the beer."

"Oh, well." She pulled the drape slightly aside, looking out the window – but there was nothing there, the street dark, empty –

The bedroom door was to Sully's right and he could hear their voices inside, creakings from the bed, bodies moving about. For a moment there was silence, then muffled voices again, bedsprings squeaking – sporadic unrhythmic noises – quiet again –

"You wouldn't have a cigarette on you, lover?"

Sully walked over to the window and gave her one. She dragged deeply, leaving the cigarette in her mouth, the smoke rising lazily past her eyes.

"Are you boys from town here?" she said. "If you don't mind me asking."

"Halifax," said Sully. For the next five minutes he told her some cock-and-bull story about his life as a sailor, the ports he'd been to around the world. He said he'd left his ship in Halifax to come up and visit friends in Saint John. The Bonaventure – "You must've heard of it, there was a show on TV about it, the big aircraft carrier? We call 'er the Bonny for short." It was sailing in a couple of days and he had to take the train back tomorrow. Paris was their next port of call, he said.

"Paris? Do ships go there?"

"Sure. What do you think?"

"Seems to me I seen it on the map — I thought it was inland."

"Yeah, but they got a river, eh? We go up the fuckin' river."

"I wish I could go to Paris. I love to travel. But I've never been anywhere much. Montreal, I was there for a few years, but that was quite a while ago. Once I was going to — " She stopped, listening. There was a rumpus going on in the bedroom. Sully turned his head. All at once the door flew open and Harris stormed out and across the room, making straight for the front hall. "Let's go, Sully," he said without looking back.

"What's your rush?"

"C'mon, let's get outa here."

"We gotta finish our beer—"

"Fuck the beer — How do I get this goddamn door open — " Sully heard him out in the hall kicking at the door, cursing. Vera shrugged, got up from her stool by the window and let him out. "That's all there is to it, love, you don't have to knock the house down—"

"What's eating him?" she said when she returned.

"Beats me," said Sully.

The other woman was still in the bedroom. Sully could hear her moving around in there. The young girl didn't look up – the knitting needles moving deftly, her fingers never stopping –

"I guess I better go too," said Sully. "I'll take this with me." He tucked Harris's quart under his belt and downed his own in a final gulp. "Well, we'll see you again someday," he said.

"Anytime. And try and bring a little of your poker winnings with you when you come."

"Right. I'll send you a postcard when I get to Paris."

"You do that, love."

Harris was standing under a streetlight halfway up Cobourg Street, waiting for him.

"You goddamn cocksucker," he said when Sully reached him.

"What's wrong? What'd you run out like that for?"

"It's all your fault."

"What's my fault? What happened?"

"Let's get the hell away from here."

They started walking towards the crest of the hill, going past a climbing row of dark clapboard houses with steep downhill sides.

"Did you bring my beer?" he said.

He took the quart from Sully and threw back his head, guzzling it until there was nothing left but foam in the bottom, and then tossed the empty over a fence. When they resumed walking he said, "You lousy prick, Sully."

"What'd I do?"

"You got me in that place. Give's a smoke. Give's a light."

He got a cigarette going, muttering all the time, "That old whore! That old whore!"

"What happened?"

"Jesus!"

"C'mon, Harris."

"That old fuckin' old whore!"

"How was it?"

"How was it? Jesus!"

At Union Street they turned right going towards Dock Street, towards the tavern where they'd left Nick and Dearborn — Harris was in a daze — walking hurriedly along, muttering — "You shoulda seen it! — God —"

Sully after some prodding got the story out of him — promising not to utter a word to Nick or Dearborn — or anyone — They stopped in front of a small Anglican church to take a breather after the climb up the hill, sitting on the low stone wall fronting the sidewalk. They were far enough from the whorehouse, Harris figured. He could stop now and collect himself.

"I hardly had a chance to think," he said. Once he got around to it the words started pouring out. "Sully, you shoulda seen it — She didn't give me no warning at all, she just hauled up her dress and flopped down on her back on the bed and said come and get it. No panties on or nothing — I nearly fainted at the sight, so help me — that big jeezus flabby gut hanging down in rolls — but the cunt!" A shudder ran through him. "I was nearly sick, I nearly puked right there, I never seen nothing like that before. She had her knees up and her legs wide open — and it was all slimy and fat and runny and with soggy gray hairs over it — I couldn't bear to look at it — like her guts falling out — and the stink! Ugh! I didn't know what in Christ to do, I was sure I was gonna puke. I just stood there trying not to gag. I would've turned and run but she'd made me give her the five bucks soon as she closed the door — So I didn't know what to do... Let's go, Sully, I don't want to think about it—"

"C'mon, what'd you do?"

"She says 'Hurry up, sonny, I ain't got all night, my time's money.' Stupid arse, I'd already give her the five dollars, and I was stuck—"

"Then what?"

"I don't want to talk about it."

"You can't stop a story in the fuckin' middle. What happened?"

"What do you *think* happened?"

"Don't ask me — You're the one was there."

"Well, I took me pants off — But fuck it, I couldn't get a hard-on — How was I supposed to get a stiff with that godawful sight in front of me? So I says, 'I don't have no hard-on.' And she says, 'Don't worry, honey, climb on and it'll come up.' So I got on top of her then, like a goddamn fool, holding my nose, and I lay there not doing nothing, and it was just the same, my tool no stiffer than a jeezly worm. Well, after a bit she shoved me off and grabbed hold of my cock and started yankin' on it, pulling on it for all she's worth — like she's trying to jerk me off — Jesus! she nearly tore it out by the roots. I had to tell her to cut it out, it wasn't helping none — it fuckin' hurt — it still hurts. I told her to stop it, I said I couldn't get a hard-on over the likes of her — her and that big stinking cunt — Jesus, that's gonna give me nightmares — 'What's wrong?' she says. 'What's the trouble?'... Nobody in the whole Christless world could raise a bone from that old bag..."

"Then what?"

"Then nothing. That was it. I got dressed and asked her for my money back. I didn't intend to give her five bucks for nothing. But she wouldn't give it to me. She just laughed — not a fuckin' tooth in her head — she said it wasn't her problem I couldn't get a hard-on. Not her fault — I'd like to know whose it was. It ain't funny, Sully. So then I asked for half it back, I said I'd settle for two-fifty but she wouldn't even give me that. She said I was paying for her time and that's what I got. I said I might've got her time but I didn't get my leather, and that's what I'd come looking for. She just told me to get the hell out."

"That's when you come bustin' out the door?"

"No, I give her a bit of a rakin' first, I told her she should be in the old folks home, not trying to peddle her arse. I said if I wanted to see sights like her I could always go to a horror show — and it'd be cheaper too. Then I beat it. I couldn't get out of there fast enough. You won't catch me in no whorehouse again. And don't tell no one, eh? Don't tell Nick, for Christsake. Tell him the broads were all too hard-looking or something so we bought a couple of beers instead and drank them and left. Okay?"

"Okay."

Shortly after, back at the tavern, Harris sat fuming through the whole story, glaring and nodding at Sully as he recounted it for the others. "Nice guy, nice guy you are, Sully. Nice guy."

"We won't tell no one else," said Nick, cackling, when Sully was finished.

"Yeah, I bet you won't."

"We won't say a word. Eh, Sully?"

"Certainly not."

"What kind of friends does he think we are, anyway?"

Later that night, when the taverns were closed, they climbed into Nick's car and drove back to Bannonbridge, stopping on the way at Fredericton to borrow a bottle from a friend of Nick's who trained horses at the racetrack there.

§

The Black Horse was a strictly functional tavern, you went there to drink, not to admire the surroundings. There was none of your exposed oak beams or muskets and powderhorns on the wall — no fireplace, no leaded windows, no finely panelled walls — just a plain rectangular room filled with standard tavern chairs and tables. The only concession to decorativeness was a massive framed print of a moose wading in a forest stream, the sort you see on calendars. Years ago, so my old man once told me, there had been dozens of taverns and bars in Bannonbridge, when the town was an active seaport. And then came a period of prohibition and they were all closed down. When the dry law was repealed government liquor stores were opened, but it was decades before taverns were again permitted, and then so begrudgingly and with so much politics involved that the Black Horse was the only one in Bannonbridge to obtain a license.

I had some change left over from the grocery shopping, enough for a glass of beer, and so to the Black Horse I went, as the logical place to spend it. I could hear Sully and Nick talking excitedly even before I opened the door. They were almost the only ones in there.

" – then we'll make a tape and send it to a record company – we'll do a tour–"

There was something smug and condescending about the way they told me the news. They were cocky, filled with a sense of their own grandeur. I could see what success would do to them, how it would turn their heads, if they were like this even now—

"So can you play anything?" Nick said. He was very businesslike.

"He can't play nothing," Sully answered for me.

What they were doing, they were getting together a band, a rock 'n roll band no less. It wasn't some farfetched idle speculation – they were in with both feet, or up to their necks –

"We have to be ready by Friday night," said Sully. This was on a Monday afternoon. "Nick's got us a dance at the high school – no shit. He set it up. Right, Nick?"

"You're damn right it's right."

"Who're you using for musicians?" I said.

"We got two right now, to start with."

"Yeah? Who are they?"

"You're looking at them."

The only other people in the tavern were Bennie Carter and Spanish Jack McIntyre — two veteran soaks who practically lived in the place —

"Jeez, I never thought those old guys—"

"Cut it out," said Sully. "Nick's on the skins and the kid's gonna do the vocals."

Now that he mentioned it Nick did own a battered-up set of drums of sorts. They'd been thrown in to round off the deal when he bought that old car of his — when the muffler fell off on the test drive. In fact I'd heard him play, it was at his place one day when no one was at home, he wanted to "show his stuff" to Sully and me — I remembered it clearly — the endless barrage of crashes and bangs, like a china shop in an earthquake —

It's true Sully's voice wasn't all that bad, you had to give him that; he could carry a tune. But I was sure he didn't know the words to any more songs than I did — which was none, not all the way through — I'd hung around him long enough to know that. He might manage a line or two, a phrase here and there, like anyone who listens to the radio from time to time, but that was about it.

"Then there's Harris," said Sully.

"The Leech?"

"He's got an electric guitar, Nick says. He never told no one."

"An amplifier too," said Nick.

"His old man — you know, always buying that junk. He got it for a song. I never heard him but Nick says he can play some."

"He can pick a little — It don't matter. He's got the amp and we gotta have it. If we can make enough noise they'll never know the difference. All you have to do is deafen the bastards, that's all they want."

"And who else beside Harris?"

"We're still hunting around. We only started in business yesterday. We got nearly a week to get ready."

How this came about is a tribute to Nick's ingenuity, if not to his integrity.

The day before he'd been sitting by himself in one of the high-backed booths in the Castle Restaurant, listening to a flock of girls chattering in the booth behind him. They belonged to the CY-High – a Catholic youth group – and they'd got permission from their director or custodian or whatever, Father Malley, the assistant parish priest, to hold a dance, after months of persuasion – but they had no money to hire a band. Thirty dollars was all they dare guarantee, in the hope the gate would cover it, which it probably would, easily; but they were new at this, they'd never organized a dance before and were afraid of risks. The only local rock group, The Ambassadors, had a flat rate of fifty dollars, as did The Schooners from Clifton, who had another engagement in any case. The dance was set for the coming Friday. Everything else was under control, the food, the chaperones, the place – they had the auditorium at St. Cecilia's High – but getting a band to play was proving to be no small problem. The alternative was to play records, which nobody wanted to do. Their hearts were set on a live band. And if the dance was a success they could have one every couple of weeks – so Father Malley had reluctantly agreed–

While Nick was absorbing all this a scheme took shape in his mind. He kept out of sight, slumped down as he was in the booth, and when the girls left he went for a walk to think things over. Half an hour later he phoned the head of the dance committee, a girl named Ellen Saunders, and said he'd heard the CY-High were holding a dance, and that they had no band to play for it. "Your worries are over," he said.

When she learned who she was talking to, she was somewhat skeptical — but then she only knew Nick by reputation, he was half a dozen years older — and they were certainly desperate. She listened with an open mind as Nick assured her his group had been practicing together for almost a year, but they hadn't been able to get any bookings because The Ambassadors and The Schooners had them all tied up. All they needed was a start — they were prepared to work at cut rates, he said, just forty dollars, because they needed the exposure —

"Well, we can only pay thirty — unless we take in more than that—"

Nick pretended disappointment. "That's not very much — it'll hardly pay for broken guitar strings—"

"We can give you half of what we make over thirty dollars, perhaps — that is — I mean, do you really have a band? I've never heard anything about it. What do you call yourselves?"

For some reason Nick hadn't thought of that.

"The — uh — Mercuries," he said.

"The Mercuries? Like the car?"

"We ain't really settled on a name yet — We're thinking about half a dozen — That's just one of them.

We'll have a real good one picked by tomorrow —
Soon's we know we're gonna be playing—"

"We have to put posters up."

"We'll have our name ready — that ain't
important, it's the music. Some bands don't even have
a name. The Ambassadors played for nearly a year
without one."

"Who's in your band?"

"Oh..." Nick was ready for this one. "We got
Allie Robinson on lead guitar—"

"You have? I thought he went to Toronto? He
used to play with the Schooners."

"I know, but he's back, and he's with us now."

"Oh — well — that's good—"

"And Lou Cowan on bass—"

"Lou Cowan?"

"Sure."

"I thought — Isn't he in the hospital? After that
accident?"

"He's out now. He's all better."

"I heard he was paralyzed."

"That's what everyone thought. But they cured
him. He's still a bit stiff, but it don't hurt his playing.
And Sully's our singer. Sullivan, you know."

"Sully?"

"Yeah — you never heard him sing? You must've
heard Sully sing. He's got a voice like Ray Charles,
something like that. You have to hear him. You'd never
believe it. I'm on the drums, myself. Sully plays rhythm
guitar too. And we're getting a guy from Moncton on
the sax — he's gonna work out with us this evening —
he's played in the States—"

"Well... it all *sounds* good—"

"Look, I'll tell you what. We're having a session tonight, we practice every night. I'll call you back in an hour or two and you can listen to us — If that don't convince you nothing will."

In a couple of hours Nick called her, with his record player pulled up close to the phone.

"We're just getting warmed up now, but we'll do something for you anyway — We get better as we go along, but this'll give you an idea. Ready?"

"Yes."

"Okay, boys. Let's go — Wait'll I get settled in here — Outa me way, Lou, for Godsake — One... two... three..." With that he put on a record by the Coasters — an obscure flipside he was sure she couldn't identify — and while the music played he hollered from the far side of the room, "Take 'er, Harris!" and moments later, "Okay, Allie!" and then a whoop — and so on — When the record was over he lifted the needle and the turntable spun silently, and he said into the phone, "Whew! You work up a sweat hammerin' them drums."

Ellen was at a loss for words — her expectations far exceeded — "I had no idea — I never dreamed you'd be that good—"

"Oh, we're not bad. We made a few mistakes there — you might've noticed there, about halfway through — we missed a beat or two—"

"I didn't notice—"

"It was nothing. We'll have 'er polished by — Friday, ain't it?"

"Yes, Friday night."

"Are we hired, then?"

"Oh, yes. You've saved our lives."

Nick sat there in the tavern, cackling quietly, gloating over his cleverness.

"What'll you do Friday, when they find out?" I asked him.

"What's there to find out? They want a band — that's what they'll get. We'll be there."

"What about Robinson and Cowan — how'll you explain that?"

"That don't matter. It'll be too late by then to make any difference. They couldn't make it — That's all I tell them — Robinson had to go back to Toronto — Cowan's not feeling too good, the paralysis come over him again — his pickin' fingers tightened up — so we got a couple of replacements. They can't do nothing about it. Once we're in, we're in. All we have to do is put on a good show."

Sully was thinking. He sat up. He had an inspiration. "I know who else we can get."

"Who?"

"There's a piano in the auditorium, right? So we got a free instrument. All we need is a guy to play it."

"Who're you thinking of`?"

"William — William Bryenton."

"William! That fuckin' fruit!"

"What's the difference? He plays the piano."

"I don't want him in my band."

"What do you mean, your band?"

"It'll give us a bad name — They'll think we're a bunch of cocksuckers."

"He's a good fuckin' piano player. He's been taking lessons since he was about two years old."

"We'd have to be watching him all the time —
he'd give you a blow-job right on the stage—"

"No, but I was thinking — there's another thing
— we need a place to practice, don't we?"

"What's that got to do with it? We can practice
anywhere."

"At your place, eh?"

"Not jeezless likely. We got boarders — I can't
even play me drums there, let alone bring in an
amplifier. I was thinking of at your house."

"Sure, the old lady'd love that. You see what I
mean? We can't use someone's house because of all
the racket. And if we're gonna have someone on piano
then there's got to be a piano wherever we go to
practice — we can't go lugging one around with us. So
that's where William fits in. His old man practically
runs the Knights of Columbus, and they got a big hall
with a piano and a pool table and everything—"

"We don't need a fuckin' pool table in the
band—"

"It's just there, I mean. We tell William to get
hold of his old man's key, see? There's never anyone
around in the daytime — I been to the place with him
a couple of times shooting pool — He was supposed to
be dusting the furniture or something."

"He can't do the kind of music we want," said
Nick. "He plays that highbrow horseshit. I heard him in
the Festival."

"He can play anything. I'm telling you."

"I dunno..." Nick, however, relented finally,
acknowledging there was something to be gained by
taking William into the band — at least temporarily —

until they could find another piano player and some other place to practice.

"We could call ourselves The Knob-gobblers," he said.

"What's the name gonna be, anyway? The Mercuries — that's no good. There's a band in Fredericton called that."

"It's all I could think of. We'll come up with something."

"Well, we got four guys now," said Sully.

"Three guys and one fag."

"Drums, guitar, piano and voice. We need more than that, we have to have a heavier sound." He said to me, "How come you don't play something? We could use another guitar, it's too bad you can't play a sax or something."

"I play hockey a bit."

"That's what we should have, a sax."

"Lend us a quarter, Sully," said Nick. "I want to get another beer."

"I don't have a quarter, I'm flat."

"Then let's get the hell outa here. We got work to do, we don't have much time to get ready. You talk to William and get that hall business arranged, we'll have our first practice tomorrow afternoon. We'll have to get a couple of wines so we can loosen out. Get that cocksucker to buy some wine, he must have lots of money."

We drained the last drops of beer and went outside onto the Front Street. The air was brisk, it was mid-November by this time — the shop roofs vivid against the sky — the sun shining. Striding along the opposite sidewalk with a preoccupied look on his face was Ralph.

"There's Ralph."

"Jesus, I forgot all about him. How stupid can you get—"

"We don't want that crazy bastard," said Nick. "A trumpet's no good to us—"

Sully hollered, "Ralph!"

"How's she goin', boys!" Ralph crossed the street to where we were. "In having a couple, eh? I can't go in there, they told me I'm not allowed in that place. I have to take my business elsewhere."

"Listen, Ralph." Sully came right to the point — He asked Ralph if he'd play for them, in their new band — He told him about the band — "A trumpet'll round things out," he said.

"I don't know, Sully — they're only teenagers, high school kids, they don't want my kind of music."

"They ain't heard us yet. You'll fit right in, the trumpet'll give us a different kind of sound — You need a new twist in this music racket—"

Ralph was sober. He turned his head away shyly, looking at his reflection in a store window.

"What the hell. You don't need to twist my arm. I don't care, sure I'll play with you, it don't make any difference to me. Why not? It's better than playing with myself — " He scuffed the ground with his toe, chuckling. "Eh, boys? It's better than playing with myself. There's no money in that. Sure I'm with you. How much are you paying?"

"Well... We're not going to make a hell of a lot this first dance, there'll be more once we're established. We can only give you—"

"Five bucks," put in Nick. "That's more than the fruit's gonna get, he ain't gettin' nothin'. And five for Harris. We got expenses."

"Holy sufferin'... Five bucks. I knew if I kept at it I'd make the big time. Shit on it, money don't mean nothing to me — the glory's enough. As long as I get the glory. Are there going to be any drinks at that dance?"

"Oh yeah, we'll have some booze," said Sully. "You'll get enough to drink."

"In that case I'll be there. As long as there's a drop to be had you won't have to worry about me not showing up."

"And we're practicing tomorrow. Can you make it?"

"Wait'll I check my schedule... Yeah, I can make it, boys — I don't think I'm tied up — I'll take the afternoon off—"

"It's at the Knights of Columbus Hall. About two o'clock."

"Okay. I'll be there."

Sully and Nick were on their way to Sully's house to phone William, and since I lived in the other direction we parted company. Ralph said he'd walk along with me for a while. "I'm not going anywhere in particular," he said, "one way's as good as another."

It was the first time I'd talked to Ralph since coming back from Saint John. I was curious about what had become of the Bishop. I hadn't noticed him around or heard anything about him.

"Oh, they sent him off to Campbellton, to the Asylum," said Ralph.

"Because of the collection box?"

"No, they didn't get him for that. His mother found a lot of stuff hidden in his room, a whole priest's rig he'd stolen, the complete outfit — like they say mass in, the cape and hat and everything — and a gold chalice, all kinds of things from the church. The poor guy can't be too right in the head when you think of it. You can understand the wine, but that other stuff... But I don't know, though. The Knights of Columbus dress up in capes and swords and they don't put them away. It depends who you are — It's okay if you're part of a crowd, and you can pay for your uniform — They don't bother you then—"

We walked past the small stores on Water Street, buildings dating from the first of the century, older than that, some of them, not changed at all on the second stories, the roofs, the eaves, the dormer windows. Where the little Chinese Laundry used to stand there was a hole now, like a missing tooth, with a low board wall across it. Going by you could see the railroad tracks and an enormous elm tree bare of leaves and a weatherbeaten old warehouse and a couple of crumbling wharves — And the river, half a mile across and deep blue, with farms on the other shore and auburn fields in the sun.

At Breen Street we cut right towards the park. Ralph was talking as we went along, telling me about his inventions. He had thirty-six inventions, he said — "I bet you didn't know that, eh? Thirty-six. You'd think they'd be worth a pile of money, but they're not worth a cent till I get them patented and I can't afford it. It costs five hundred dollars to get a patent... I'll never have that kind of money. What do you think of this? It's one of my inventions — for going in the woods, in case you get lost. Even if you don't get lost it's still a handy gadget to have. It looks like a jackknife, it's got a blade and a can opener and a bottle opener – but here's the difference – it's got a small flashlight built into it, and a cigarette lighter, and a compass – everything you need to survive – and it's all one piece and not much bigger than your ordinary jackknife. What do you think of that? You suppose that'd sell?"

"It sounds pretty useful – Sure, why not?"

"I've got lots of inventions. Thirty-six. I'm always thinking up new ones. Here's another one. It looks like a little ferris wheel, you put it on the table and the seats hold things like candies or cookies, and you press a lever and it goes around, and you can stop it at the kind of goody you like. That'd be a neat little gadget, eh? Kids'd really like that. What do you think? I could send the plans away to a company – some place that manufactures toys, only I don't have any patents. With no patents they could just go ahead and use my ideas and not pay me a penny. They'd get their own patents for them... I can't take the chance. Here's another one. It goes on a kid's bike, it's a flashlight but there's a transistor radio in it. That's a good idea, eh? The kids would like that, they could ride around and listen to the radio, and at night they'd have a light on their bikes at the same time. That'd sell well. Some company that makes toys, they'd love to have that. But I need a patent first... You have to send a drawing away and they do a search, and if it's the only one of its kind they register it... Then you can sell the rights to some company. I wrote to find out about it, I saw an ad in a magazine, and they wrote back telling me the cost. Just the search alone costs a hundred dollars.

They have to find out if somebody else had the same idea ahead of you. If that's the case you come away with nothing — You lose your money and you're left with nothing to show for it. But if it's a new idea then there's more expense, your patent application — it adds up. Even then, once you've got the patent you still have to find a company that'll buy your invention... People think there's nothing to it... They figure if you've got a good invention you'll get rich right away. Shit, I can't even afford to get the search done — I can't even afford a pint of beer. I have to go bumming around the streets to get enough to drink."

"Well, there's always the band you're in now, Ralph. There might be some money in that. Maybe you guys'll go places."

"Go places, all right. They don't know anything about music, those guys, the only place we'll go is out the door once the kids hear what we sound like. We might have to go places, before they put the boots to us. I shouldn't be letting myself in for this. I must be crazy. I don't see why I should make a fool of myself—"

"Well, you're in it now. You're not going to change your mind, are you?"

"Oh, I'll go along with them. If the drinks are free they'll have to bar the door if they want to keep me out. Five dollars they're paying me... Hah!"

We crossed the park diagonally and when we reached the bench in front of the war memorial Ralph said he'd see me later.

"I'm going to sit here for a while and think how I'll invest that money. A big decision like that requires a lot of hard thinking. I guess it'll be four quarts of wine – But I haven't had a drink of rum for a while – Or maybe a couple of cases of beer – I'll see you tomorrow – They'll probably never pay me anyway –"

§

If the band could have heard themselves, if they'd had a tape recorder and played back their rehearsal, they'd never have showed up for the dance Friday night; they'd have gone and hid themselves somewhere. I was their only audience and it was all I could do to keep from bursting out laughing. I had to bite my tongue. On the wall there was a stuffed moose head and even that had a grin on its face.

The wine must have affected their ears, the three bottles of Napoleon we had. When Ralph saw the label he said, "I drank a lot of that with the Bishop. Napoleon! He's supposed to be dead – everyone thinks he's dead but I'm still fighting him – "

Ralph had a kind of wry look on his face; he wasn't deceived; and William surely wasn't. But the others, they were in love with the noise they made, delighted with it, like one of their own farts, like a baby with its own shit. Harris was the worst, even worse than Nick. Because of his amplifier everything he did was magnified, and it was only an accident when he hit the right note. The amplifier kept letting out ear-piercing squeals and screeches – a feedback problem – and he was up and down like a jack-in-the-box adjusting knobs and bawling at the others to stop and wait till he was ready. When he bobbed up and put his guitar into the fray again you could tell right off he didn't know one string from another –

Nor was Sully much help. He hadn't learned the words to even a single song, not one he could do from start to finish. He came close with "Hound Dog" and "Whole lotta shakin' goin' on", and he had one verse and the chorus to "Blueberry Hill" down pat. But beyond that he had to hum the missing lines or fill them in with gibberish. It didn't help much that Ralph and William were able to play their instruments – they only highlighted the incompetency of the others – confused what would otherwise have been flawless discord. Ralph's version of "Tequila" began well, until his solo lead-in was suddenly hit by a cacophonous onslaught from the background. He put his trumpet down after a few more bars and said, "Piss on that, I need a drink."

"C'mon, Ralph, keep playing – It sounds the very best–"

"You guys play, you don't need me."

William's piano was just audible but Sully could be heard well enough, with the few lyrics he knew. He had a hand mike plugged into the amplifier. When they started another song the amplifier squealed with pain – It put your teeth on edge – And the rest of that noise – the pandemonium – anyone passing on the street must have wondered about the Knights of Columbus, what they were up to in there. William kept casting nervous glances towards the door. When they were finished that particular number he said, "Oh dear, I don't know... If daddy finds out we're here he'll kill us." He'd lifted the key to the hall from his father's desk at home, where he kept a spare.

"Don't worry about it," said Sully. "Have a drink."

"I don't think I ought to — mummy might smell it on my breath—"

"Go ahead, take a slug."

William took a tentative nip from the bottle and made a face. "Jeepers!"

He was thrilled they'd asked him to play in their band, that they'd actually asked him — It was a new experience, he'd never been out and about before, running around with the boys — He was full of new sensations —

"Lets take a break," said Sully.

"Naw, let's keep at it," said Nick.

"Time for a break," said Ralph. "We don't want to wear ourselves out."

"Yeah, my fingers are getting sore," said Harris.

So they all left their instruments and flopped into the big leather easy chairs.

"You got those names ready yet?" said Nick to me. I was still scribbling them down, my list of ideas. I added a few more, then tore the sheets from my notebook so they could have a look and make their choice. They were just things that popped into my head, I didn't try too hard, as you'll see. The list went like this:

NAMES FOR THE BAND

The Winners
The Losers
The Sinners
The Cruisers
The Boozers
The Contenders

The Offenders
The Outsiders
The Insiders
The Petitions
The Seditions
The Contritions
The Intolerable Conditions
The Bannonbridge Musicians
The Bad Band
The Sad Band
The Mad Band
The Apocalypse
The Potato Chips
The Disaster
The Fallen Lumps of Plaster
Nix Six
Nick's Dicks
The Plague
The Bloody Rag
Sully's Folly
Sully and the Follies
William and the Willies
Ralph and the Rubbies
Harris and the Embarrassments
Harris's Bare Arse
The Band that Shook the World
The Filthy Five
The Fearless Five
The Ferocious Five
The Atrocious Five
The Dreamers
The Schemers
The Wieners

The Five Knobs
The Ten Balls
The Five and Ten
The Circus
The Acrobats
The Alleycats
The Clowns
The Sideshow
The Trapeezers
The Beezers
The Sneezers
The Five Sleazers
The Lemon Squeezers
The Be-Jeezers
The Darts
The Spare Parts
The Five Farts
The Quarts
The Five Warts
The Quick Retorts
The Dirty Old Shorts
The Snorts
The Grunts
The Daring Stunts
The Five Cunts
The Ants
The Impossible Chance
The Last Stance
The Rip in the Pants
The One Night Stand
The Worst in the Land
A Bird in the Hand
Five Birds in Five Hands

Nick and his Prick
Sully and his Bare Belly
Harris and the View from the Terrace
Ramsay's Lambsies
William and the Vermillion Pavillion
The Leechers
The Preachers
The First Features
The Creatures
The Hawks
The Wrong Pair of Socks
The Eagles
The Beagles
The Evil-Eye Fleagles
The Sensations
The Hesitations
The Incubations
The Menstruations
The Masturbations
The Premature Ejaculations

With so many names to choose from they had a tough time making their decision. There were some they didn't care for – as they read down the list – things like The Bad Band – "What do you mean, bad band, we're fuckin' good – " "What's this, The Apo... calypso – what in hell's that supposed to mean? The Disaster – for Christ's sake–"

"Nick's Six. That ain't bad," said Nick.

"Where's the jeezless six, we're only five –"

"I counted myself," I said. "So it'd rhyme–"

"Yeah, but you won't be up there playing. They'll think we can't count," said Sully.

"It's a good name, though," said Nick.

"Sully and the Follies! Jesus, why not call it Sully and the Fairies and get it over with!"

"How about something like — Sully and the Rockets," said Sully.

"Take a walk, Jack — you're not the head—"

"I'm the singer, you're supposed to call it after the singer. Like Bill Haley and the Comets — Buddy Hollie and the Crickets — Gene Vincent and the Bluecaps — They all do that—"

"Ralph and the Rubbies—"

"Harris's Bare Arse — that's a good one—"

"William and the—"

"We ain't gettin' no William in there," said Nick.

"Oh, I don't want—"

"You're goddamn right you don't want."

"The Filthy Five — Come out of that—"

"The Dreamers don't sound too bad."

"There was one back there — let's see — The Hawks, that sounds good —

"The Five Knobs—"

"The Clowns — that's us all right—"

"Naw, we can't use that, this ain't no joke."

"The Acrobats sounds pretty good."

"Go 'way, Harris. What're you gonna do, hang by your toes while you play?"

"It's just a name, we don't have to do tricks—"

"That's no good of a name."

"The Darts — how about that?"

"Yeah, that don't sound too bad."

"The Five Farts—"

"The Dirty Old Shorts — you must be fuckin' crazy—"

"The Five Cunts — that'd go over big with Father Malley."

"Hmm, Jesus..." Sully mimicked Father Malley's ponderous, pompous voice. "Music by The Five Cunts, is it? I don't believe I've heard of that band—"

"These are too goddamn strange."

"Well, we gotta get something. Some of them ain't that bad. The first one, what about The Winners?"

"Yeah, that don't sound too bad. The Cruisers — naw—"

"The Outsiders — that's good — or that other one, the Darts—"

"The One Night Stand," said Ralph. "That's the right one."

The name they finally settled on was The Creatures — because by coincidence Nick and Sully both mentioned it in the same breath, as a possibility, their eyes running down the list together. It was like a revelation, happening like that. Neither of them had to give in to the other's opinion, they both could have their way. They had to use it. It ended the bickering and harmony prevailed.

"Yeah, it's got kind of an outer space sound," said Sully. "That'll go over good."

"I seen worse," said Nick. "Okay, let's get back at it."

"It's too late — we done enough for one day. We can hit 'er another butt tomorrow."

"I don't think we should stay any longer," said William.

"Let's shoot some pool."

"We better think about getting some more to drink," said Ralph. "This stuff's almost gone. We don't need any more practice. I don't think we can get much worse."

"C'mon, Ralph. You can't look at it that way."

"You better learn some of those songs, Sullivan," said Nick.

"Don't get your water hot, I'll learn them. I know most of them already – I just have to brush up my memory–"

"All you know is about two, if you know that many."

"Go 'way with you, I know more than that. I'll think of some others. I'll get a songbook tomorrow."

"Do we have to use the Hall again?" said William.

"You're damn right. We got nowhere else to go. We'll come here every day till the dance, we got a lot of work to do."

"But daddy might find out–"

"Fuck daddy. Tell him we're here, what difference does it make? We're not hurting anything."

"He'd never let us – he'd be afraid we'd break something–"

"Well, just hope he's got better things to do than come sniffing around where he's not wanted. Ain't the old bastard working? If you got his key he won't be able to get in."

"He comes up from the store sometimes to check. He'd hear us." William's father owned a dry goods store.

"We'll worry about that tomorrow."

"I can't make it tomorrow," said Harris. "The old man's taking the truck to Bathurst and I have to go with him–"

"What? You cocksucker – " squawked Nick. "You get down here tomorrow, you can't play that fuckin' thing anyway, you need the practice more than anyone."

"I can't. Jesus, Nick – it ain't my fault – The old man's picking up a couple of fridges and I have to help him. But you can have the amplifier, I can leave it with you–"

"You're goddamn right we can have the amplifier."

"Well," Harris grumbled. "If it wasn't for me you wouldn't have one..."

"What do you want – us to kiss your arse? You better not miss the next jeezless practice."

"I won't miss any more."

"And bring a wine with you next time, too. We ain't running a free bar around here."

"I'll get one, the old man'll give me five bucks for lending him a hand."

"Don't forget. The rest of yez, then, tomorrow at two... Why don't we leave these Christless things, it's too much trouble loading them in the car."

"Oh, we can't – The Knights are here every evening," said William. "There's always someone coming in."

With a good deal of grousing out of Nick we got the drums dismantled and out to his car, and we loaded Harris's amplifier in with them. It was Tuesday – the dance was to be on Friday.

As things turned out they'd had all the practices they were going to have. They were as ready as they were going to be.

§

The band was more than a little oiled when I got down to the Knights of Columbus Hall next afternoon. I was late, I'd had to go to a class, but they'd managed to start their playing without me, only what they were playing was *pool*, their instruments sitting idle to one side. William obviously was having a few himself, miscuing and squealing and giggling. He was partnered with Nick, and Ralph was with Sully.

"Your turn, Ralph."

"What's that, Nick?"

"Your shot. C'mon, you're holding up the game."

"Oh. Sorry, boys. What am I shooting at?"

"The high balls."

"Which ones are those again?"

"The ones with the stripes on them."

"Oh. Right. Which one do you want me to shoot at, Sully?"

"Any fuckin' one. Try for the twelve, it's right over the pocket."

"The twelve. Where's that? Which one's that, Sully?"

"Right there."

"Oh. Okay, I'll try that one. The twelve. Maybe I'd better aim for the eleven if I want to put the twelve in. I'll never make this shot, Sully. I don't know how to play this game. I can't even see. Here goes." Holding the cue awkwardly he shoots and hits the twelve, but on the wrong side, and it goes knocking among the other balls.

"Good try anyway, Ralph."

"Thanks, Sully."

Ralph drifted away from the table and sat down in one of the easy chairs. "This is the life, eh boys? We should join the Knights of Columbus. Nice comfortable chairs they got here. A pool table. Darts. Big poker table. We should have a club of our own like this." He uncapped a bottle of wine that was standing on the floor beside his chair. "The Knights of Napoleon. You don't mind if I have a drink of this, Sully?"

"Go ahead. It's on William."

It was Nick's shot and he made one of the low balls, then another one, then missed by a few inches on a bank shot.

"That's it, game over," said Sully. "I'm cleaning the table." He had an easy shot on the ten, straight on the pocket. He blasted the cueball at it – a dramatic slambang – the same every shot, ten times harder than he had to – and the ball hit the back of the pocket and went flying off the table like a bullet, ricocheted off the wall and crashed through the glass door of a trophy cabinet.

William's fingers flew to his mouth –

"That did it," said Ralph.

"Nice goin', Sully. Nice shot," said Nick.

Sully laughed. "Spot 'er up."

"What'll we do? Daddy'll kill us–"

"Don't worry about it. He won't know who did it," said Sully. "Whose shot is it? It's your shot."

"Oh – jeepers! – Sully, I don't think–"

"Stop shaking. Have a drink. There's nothing we can do about it now — we might as well finish the game."

"We're supposed to be practicing our music," said Nick, "not fuckin' the dog. We better get our practice in and then clear out."

"There's no sense practicing without Harris. We can't get that damn amp to work, it won't stop screeching. Harris's the only one needs practice anyway. Here, William, take a snort."

The bottle made the rounds, and then Sully said, "Okay, spot 'er up, Nick."

"Spot 'er up yourself."

"I'm liable to cut me fingers." Sully reached gingerly into the cabinet and extracted the ball from the broken glass.

"Sully, we shouldn't stay here, I'm worried now," said William.

"You're always worried. Relax. It's your shot."

Reluctantly William aimed the cue, the point dithering nervously this way and that, his small hand resting flat on the table, forming virtually no pivot at all. "What'll I say if he finds out..."

"Put the four in," said Nick.

"Hit 'er hard," said Sully.

"Nice and easy," said Nick.

"I don't think I can do it... I'm shaking too bad..."

He drew the cue well back and held his breath and let fly. The tip cut under the ball and caught the cloth —

They all looked at him.

"Oh dear — I didn't mean to do that." There was a six inch tear in the green baize.

"That stuff only costs about ten bucks an inch," said Nick. "They'll need a whole new cloth now."

"God, you're stupid, William," said Sully.

"I didn't—"

"Look — don't tell your old man nothing about us," said Nick. "Don't say who was with you. That's all."

"Say you don't know nothing about it. None of us was here."

"He'll know it was me — He's the only one who has a key, besides Father Malley — and Mr. Reinsborough—"

"How's he gonna know? Anyway, if he finds out say you done it all by yourself."

"I didn't break the glass — Why should I take all the blame—" William was on the point of tears, really upset —

"I got an idea," said Sully. "We can leave a window open and make it look like some kids broke in. They'll think some kids done it. They're always breaking into places."

Sully went to a window and tried to open it, but it was painted in solid. He tried another one and found the same thing. He considered a moment, shrugged, and left the main room; we could hear his footsteps receding towards the back of the building. "They're all stuck," he hollered back. There was a silence, followed by a crash, not unlike the ten ball hitting the trophy case. When he returned Sully was swinging his cue nonchalantly. "They broke in back there. Okay, let's haul arse."

"You crazy bastard," said Nick. He started dismantling his drums. Sully and I got a grip on the huge amplifier and began lugging it towards the door.

"Help me with these. C'mon, don't stand there looking stupid. You – ya jeezless fruit."

"Nick – jeepers–"

"C'mon, gimme a hand. Get busy."

§

On the afternoon of the dance I was at Sully's; his mother was out and we had the house to ourselves. We were drinking vodka. Sully was less concerned than you might have expected, considering The Creatures had been able to get in just the one practice. Harris and Nick were the band's weakness, he said. The trouble with Harris was he didn't know how to play the guitar – that was all – he was just a beginner and probably tone deaf anyway –

"And Nick makes too goddamn much racket. If he'd just keep the beat he'd be okay, but he thinks he's playing a solo the whole time."

He figured the rest of the group could take up the slack. "If those two can hold 'er down some and keep in the background, and William plays that Jerry Lee Lewis style, really pumpin' the piano, with yours truly belting out the words – And Ralph doing some instrumentals, him and William – It mightn't be perfect, but when you consider the notice we had, eh? You can't get ready in less than a week like that, there's bound to be some rough edges." Everything considered it needn't turn out bad, he said. They might get lucky, it all might fall into place. You never could tell.

The fact their repertoire was on the limited side didn't appear to worry him. The solution to that was long pauses between songs. Besides which there'd be the mid-dance break, when they served the lunch. And if they played everything twice, and some things three times –

He'd memorized the words to five songs, and there were half a dozen instrumentals the other lads should be able to get through. Beyond that point they could play it by ear. They could always turn it over to William, he knew lots of tunes – they'd fill in with something–

William had been over to see Sully Thursday morning, after the damage at the Knights of Columbus had been discovered. His father had phoned the cops, in a terrible rage about it, said the Hall was a shambles. Break, enter and theft! Vandalism! William heard him make the call. Everything broken, ripped, scraped, burnt and demolished! The thieves had come in through the window and wrecked the place, taking God knows what all with them when they left. Ashtrays thrown about, chairs mutilated, table lamps shattered, carpets slashed – the Hall had been sacked, to listen to his old man – the pool table damaged beyond repair – trophies missing –

"Daddy's so worked up he's imagining things," said William. "We didn't steal anything, did we?"

"There was nothing there worth taking," said Sully. "What would we want with their goddamn trophies? Nobody'd buy those things."

Sully was holding Harris's booze for him until after supper – two pints of vodka – and that's what we were drinking. Harris had been reluctant to take them home for fear of his mother searching him; she'd done it another time, catching him on the way to his room with a quart of wine; she'd be particularly suspicious knowing about the dance tonight. "She'd be able to tell from the look on my face – she knows me too good," he said. Sully was pretty sure Harris had never drunk vodka before and wouldn't notice that his two pints were largely diluted with water – about eight parts water to one part vodka –

"He'll be mixing the stuff anyway, he'll never know the difference. We don't want him getting too drunk – he's got no capacity, Harris – We can't have him playing any worse than he does."

They were all going to be drinking hard stuff that night, The Creatures, out of pop bottles for the sake of appearance. They'd come up with the money thanks to a strategy of Nick's. He'd convinced the committee that "one of the amps needed a new transformer" or else the show was off, they wouldn't be able to play – they had to have a twenty dollar advance to cover the cost. It was too late to think of getting another band, even supposing such could be had – so the girls scraped the money together and gave it to him. You couldn't argue about equipment failures, things like this happened.

At these high school dances there was usually a lunch provided for the halfway break, the girls bringing sandwiches and cakes and cookies. It was free, part of your admission price, and they'd have a canteen set up where you could buy pop to flush it down with. Sully had an idea. We were sitting there, drinking and listening to the radio, we had time to kill — It was a notion he'd had before, we'd talked about it, but never put it into practice — Now it came back to him — We would make a sandwich —

When he first said it I didn't understand his intention.

"To take to the dance. You know the kind, like we were gonna do."

It took us a full half hour to construct the thing, rummaging about the kitchen — putting this and that between the slices of bread — mustard, ketchup, mayonnaise, dill pickle, sweet pickle, onion, nutmeg, sugar, vinegar, baking soda, mazola oil, lard, salt, pepper, flour, raw bacon, jam, tobacco, red pepper, orange peel, lemon peel, banana peel, potato peel, salt pork, cabbage, mouldy cheese, garlic, peanut butter, grass from the lawn, sand, assorted weeds, birch bark, sawdust, tea leaves and coffee grounds — a little of everything. It was somewhat thicker than your average sandwich — but some people like them that way —

"Well, I can't think of anything else," I said. I was keeping a list — the recipe — so we could show it around later.

Sully wasn't satisfied however. Now that we'd gone this far he felt it needed an added something to round it off. "Just a sec," he said. He took the sandwich and went into the bathroom, and after a few minutes came out, glowing like a chef with his *piece de resistance*, holding it at arms length.

"Oh, no..."

"Where's the list." He scribbled the last two ingredients on it.

"That's going too far. We're liable to kill somebody."

"It was only a dash of each. Just enough for the flavour."

The only flaw in our creation was that it looked by this time slightly bedraggled and disreputable, with all the handling it had got. But Sully didn't think that mattered.

"Those starvin'-eyed bastards'll be grabbing the grub so fast they'll never notice," he said. He cut it into four quarters – I let him do that, not wanting to touch it at this stage – and put it in a paper bag. Then we poured ourselves another vodka and returned to the livingroom, pissing ourselves laughing, picturing the look on the face of the victim – dumbstruck, turning green, caught between swallowing it or spitting the whole mouthful out on the floor. It gives you an idea of Sully's state of mind with such a big event in his life only hours away –

Drinking Harris's booze was an old trick of Sully's, he'd pulled it before, and Harris never found out – which is why he trusted him with the vodka. It was orange gin last time. Sully drank all that except an inch in the bottom and refilled the bottle with orange pop, adding a little vinegar and red pepper sauce to give it some bite. "It was the first time Harris tried orange gin," said Sully, when he told me about it. "The old man and old lady were at a card party or something that night and we sat right here and Harris drank the pint all by himself. I had half a dozen beers, I told him I didn't want to mix beer and gin, it might make me sick. The greedy fucker was glad to hear that, having the whole pint to himself. He kept mixing it with orange, the same stuff that was already in the bottle, and bragging about how he could handle his liquor. He hardly felt a thing, he said. Oh, he was getting a little high, he said, but not like a normal person — most guys didn't know how to handle it, they'd be laid out on the floor after a whole pint, but not him, gin was his drink — as though he'd ever had it before. You talk about proud — he couldn't stop bragging. I almost bust a gut trying to keep a straight face."

Around four-thirty, with Sully's mother due back any minute, we filled Harris's vodka pints with water and glued the seals back on — Sully had steamed them off — and I said I'd see him at the dance.

"Make sure you fix it up so I get in free," I said.

"No trouble — I'll tell them you're our manager. You can help carry in the drums or something. It don't matter. I'll arrange it at the door. Come up on the stage when you get there, we'll have our own private bar set up."

§

You could hear them even if you couldn't see them: feet stomping around on the hollow stage, a tinkling run on the piano, the rattle and thump of drums, the screech of the amplifier misfiring, a hoot of laughter, Harris cursing. The eyes of the crowd were fixed on the stage; it was a quarter after nine and they were getting restless. Nobody could fathom why the curtain was down. There were a few hollers for the music to start, for the band to reveal themselves.

Out on the floor the level of noise increased, a couple of hundred voices babbling all at once. The crowd burgeoned out from the entrance like a river delta, flowing towards the stage. It was a house beyond all expectations, they came in singly, by couples, whole groups at a time filling up the auditorium. It happened to be the only dance around that night, and everyone wanted to hear the new band anyway. Sully had remembered to tell the girls at the ticket table about my special status so I was waved by, they didn't charge me. I hung around inside the entrance a while, taking things in. The red, white and blue crepe bunting dangling from the ceiling, the hordes of teenagers pouring through the door, wandering from place to place, the girls making for the ring of chairs around the walls. The chatter, the hubbub, the movement, the smell of the school tinged with perfume and cigarette smoke. The band warming up in the background. A faded rustic scene on the canvas stage curtain. Down the left wall a knot of chaperones sat near the food table drinking tea and munching on cakes and chatting amongst themselves. Every so often they glanced apprehensively towards the door when some particularly rowdy-looking young drunks swaggered in. I noticed right off that the long table mounded with sandwiches and cakes was under guard, a girl standing at each end, arms folded, keeping a sharp look out. I'd have to try later. I had the sandwich in a paper bag in my pocket.

I popped down to the toilet for a leak. A half dozen young guys with pegged pants and duck's-arse hairdos were there, passing a quart of wine around and lighting up smokes.

"They got Ralph Ramsay playing for them, I seen him come in."

"That oughta be something."

"I dunno, I heard they're pretty good."

"What're they gonna do, stay behind the curtain all night?"

I wanted to witness the band's magnificent opening from the floor, like everyone else, but it seemed they were never going to get underway. The noises they were making sounded anything but promising. In fact it was complete chaos and confusion back behind the curtain. I found out as soon as I went up on stage – I couldn't wait any longer – that it was utter havoc. They were drunk already, the lot of them, shouting, cursing, laughing, completely at sea, fussing with the amplifier, pouring drinks into pop bottles. Orders and counter orders flying every which way.

I saw that Dearborn was with them, standing in the wings, looking on with a broad grin. When I went over to him he said he'd been assigned to raise the curtain. That was how they were going to start the show off, when they got around to it – the curtain climbing as they launched into their first number, the band playing, the curtain going up, and when The Creatures were exposed in all their glory Sully was to burst into song – A cheer would erupt – The band off and running! All very imaginative and dramatic – They'd start with "Hound Dog", Dearborn thought, something that would curl their hair – electrify their spines – or maybe it was "Whole lotta shakin' goin' on" with William pumping like mad on the piano; he wasn't sure which. He was just supposed to haul the curtain rope on signal, that's all he knew.

The amplifier made another of its piercing squeals. Harris was bent double over it, fiddling with the buttons, muttering. "This goddamn fuckin' thing — it worked all right before—"

"Plug the mike in. We better test the mike."

"Fuck the mike, it works."

"The volume, get the volume right."

"I know the volume. Lemme try again." He stood up and there was a long painful Screeeeellllll! "Goddamn..." He plucked a string on the guitar and it rang through a blitz of static — He stooped and adjusted the knobs again, and made another try — It was enough to loosen your fillings.

"Turn that down some," hollered Nick. "They won't be able to hear nothing else." He was sitting behind his drums with a coke bottle in his hand. He raised it and sucked it dry. "Where's the rum? Where's the fuckin' rum?" He let loose a flourish on the drums. "Let's get the jeezly show on the road!"

"C'mon, you guys, it's almost nine-thirty," said Sully.

"Piss on it, what's your hurry? Let them wait... They'll thank us for it later!" Ralph was off by himself near the red velveteen backdrop, slouched in a chair, his legs crossed. "Holy sufferin'... Give them their money back... " He was drinking straight rum. "Carnegie Hall..."

"I have to get this goddamn guitar tuned right," said Harris. "It's gotta be tuned right with the piano." He plucked a string again, and this time the volume wasn't quite so loud. "That'll do, eh, boys? That's okay, Nick?"

"What the fuck. Leave it. We can't fool around all night."

"Play C there, William. Wake up. Look at him – he's drunk already."

William hit a note, tittering, and they alternated on C until Harris decided he was close enough, then he set about getting his other strings in tune. While they were at their preparations I got my hands on a pint and knocked back a few good drinks and rolled a smoke. The clock was ticking on – The crowd understandably was growing restive. Beyond the curtain a voice bellowed out, "What's the hold-up? Where's the music?"

A couple of others joined in.

"Yeah! Hurry up! We can't wait all night!"

"Give us some music!"

"Get the show on the road!"

"Tell them to fuck off," said Nick.

Sully stuck his head around the end of the curtain and there was a sudden cheer. "We're going to start in exactly one minute," he announced. "Keep your shirts on."

"Let's have the music!"

Sully drew his head back inside. "We better start playing, they're getting impatient. Is everybody ready? Dearborn, you ready?"

Dearborn's face was framed by a little window where the curtain raiser looks out. He nodded.

"Put the bottles down, and don't drink in the middle of a song," said Nick.

"C'mon, Ralph, get up, are you playing tonight or not?"

"Sure I'm playing. What do you think I came here for, the rum?"

Ralph got to his feet.

"Over here, stand by the piano."

"Anywhere at all. It's all the same to me. I'll stand on top of it if you want."

"Right there, beside William, so you can hear him. Hey, is my mike plugged in?" He blew into it. "Plug it in." While Harris was inserting the plug Sully said, "Now you all got it straight what we're gonna start off with? You ready, Nick?"

"Sure. Shutup and let's get going."

"I'll give the signal, Dearborn," said Sully. "When I nod you raise the curtain."

From outside: "C'mon, start the goddamn music!"

"What's the hold-up?" The discontent was spreading.

Nick barked, "One – two – three–" and hit the drums a few fairly light slaps, William trilled on the piano, Sully nodded at Dearborn in the window, the drums grew louder, the piano plunked a little harder, the murmuring outside died down – and the curtain didn't move.

"Dearborn, for fucksake–"

"It won't go up! It's stuck." Dearborn wasn't smiling, an expression of strain on his face – He was pulling on the rope for all he was worth –

"Holy old – Stop, stop playing!"

The music ceased, and there was almost dead silence for a second – everyone on the dance floor had been waiting – in a state of suspension – and now a roar of outrage left their lips. Sully quickly looked around the curtain and shouted, "The curtain's stuck! We'll have it fixed right away!"

"We want music!"

"I said the goddamn curtain's stuck! Don't fill your pants—"

"Music! We want music!"

I'd been standing offstage not far from Dearborn, and I tried to help him with the curtain. The others got there too, and we were all grabbing at ropes and tugging but the curtain wouldn't budge an inch.

"Let me look," said William. "I think I know how it works... I was in a play once... "

"Let him look," said Sully, back from his exchange with the mob. "For Christsake, we can't play from behind the curtain."

"Why not? I think we should leave it this way," said Ralph. "It's something to hide behind. I think we should all go home."

"Here, see? This rope is wound around a peg up here." William unwound one of the silken cords. "Try it now, Dearborn." Dearborn gave a pull. "Harder, it's heavy." The curtain rose suddenly, about a yard off the stage. The crowd whistled and applauded.

"Okay, put it down and let's start over," said Sully. When the curtain dropped with a thump there was a great moan from the crowd.

I heard Ralph mutter as he went by me, "What the hell...What're we playing, anyway? I can't remember all this stuff."

Sully poked his head around the curtain and announced, "It's all set now!" and drew it back quickly.

"Everyone ready?"

Nick began, "One – two – three – " And they led off with the same mesh of piano and drums, the crowd of teenagers hooting and cheering again. The curtain ascended in a stuttering fashion, about two feet with each of Dearborn's pulls. The noise on the floor subsided. All eyes were turned to the stage. William and Nick were building to the point where the full band would plunge into "Hound Dog" with their combined force – Sully stood expectantly with the microphone near his mouth – he turned and nodded to Harris and then to Ralph, alerting them – the curtain was almost to the top – Ralph had his trumpet to his lips – this was it – As one man the band stormed into their first number with unparalleled gusto – enormous enthusiasm, all stops pulled out –

It couldn't have been worse. The crowd stood stunned. In the general disarray Ralph had got his songs confused, instead of playing "Hound Dog" he was blasting out with "Whole lotta shakin' goin' on" – they were playing two different pieces at once! It would have been bad enough anyway – but this – I was afraid Dearborn would let the curtain drop, he was standing in his window holding the rope laughing, shaking helplessly, tears in his eyes. A tremendous guffaw went up from the crowd. They'd never heard such a noise before, such discordancy, such a blatant racket –

I could hear Sully shouting urgently through it all, "Change! Change!"

"Holy old dyin'..." Ralph lowered his trumpet in disgust. "What're you guys doing–"

"We're supposed to be playing 'Hound Dog'," squealed William.

"Why didn't you say so? I can't tell what you guys are playing."

Sully was bawling at Harris, "Switch to 'Whole lotta shakin'!" They had more or less ground to a halt by now. "Quick! Okay, again! One – two – three – " This time the others started "Whole lotta shakin' goin' on" and Ralph, correcting himself, blared in with "Hound Dog" – It was the same mess, only in reverse. William took his hands off the keys and turned on his stool and looked at the others in bewilderment. Nick put his sticks down – He reached for his bottle and gulped a big drink – "Aw, yez're all crazy–"

"Fuck it!" said Sully. "Stop!" He had the microphone to his mouth, but the "fuck" didn't carry beyond the stage – it wasn't working, though he didn't know it yet – "Stop! Let's get organized!" They regrouped – They took their time about it – The crowd gradually calmed some – I could see they weren't overjoyed by the performance so far, not all of them. The committee girls were looking pretty sour – And the chaperones had their heads together. They must have known it would come to this, the music kids listened to today. Some minutes later the band was ready to try again. This time there'd be no mistake, everyone had it straight what the song was going to be – One, two, three – They were off – Sully's mouth moving like a mimic –

"We can't hear you! Sing louder!"

"Turn your mike on!"

Sully couldn't be heard more than a few feet away, if that. He didn't understand for a while. He kept singing with the microphone dead as a doornail. The piano was lost in Harris's frenzied off-key picking and Nick's bedlamic hammering on the drums. After a few bars Ralph quit, but the song got played through to the end – whatever it was – nobody but the band knew, it was impossible to decipher – just an ungodly din –

When they finished there was a raucous caricature of applause from the drunks on the floor, then a more general grumbling of disapproval from those who'd come to dance – You could pick out the committee girls by the looks of disgust on their faces, the embarrassment, the anger – The Creatures decided they'd better take a break and talk things over – They withdrew to the back of the stage –

"We might as well pack it up and go home," said Ralph.

"They'd have our balls. We can't back out now."

"We ain't quitting," said Nick. "They still owe us money. If we pull out they won't pay us."

"I can't sing without a mike. Can't you fix that thing, Harris?"

"It worked okay last time I tried it. I don't know what's wrong."

"We'll have to stick to instrumentals till we get it working."

"Piss on it all. We're just making fools of ourselves."

"Pour that offstage, Ralph. Don't let the chaperones see you."

When Ralph was ready to play he said he would do "Tequila" but with the provision that only William accompany him. The others could take a rest, he said. "All I want is the piano – You know that one, William?"

"You need drums, for Jesussake," said Nick.

"I don't want any drums. I don't need drums."

"I can pick that," said Harris.

"The hell with it, then," said Ralph.

"You couldn't pick your nose, Harris," said Sully. "Get busy and fix that mike. That's what you should be doing."

"Jeez, I can play that one."

"I'll do a solo in the middle," said Nick.

"Let him do it alone," said Sully. "We gotta do something right. Let him play it the way he wants — We're in a jeezless mess with no mike—"

It was the difference between night and day, Ralph and William playing unhindered. They gave a flawless rendition. Couples even got up and began dancing. The mood of the place changed, and when they finished the applause was genuine. The band instantly cheered up; it seemed they weren't so bad after all.

"See — We can handle 'er," said Sully.

They tried their best to repair the microphone; they did everything they could — pulled the plug out and blew on it and plugged it in again — examined the wire for breaks — shook the mike, banged it on the floor, stared at it, cursed it — but nothing worked. It looked as though Sully was through for the night, without having even begun. He pulled up a chair beside me in the wings and pondered while the band did an instrumental — an atrocious attempt at "Kansas City" with Harris supposedly leading the way. A few couples tried to dance, getting all balled up — the beat gone haywire, the musicians playing at cross purposes, oblivious to each other — one by one the dancers stopped. Then Sully hit on an idea. When "Kansas City" finished he instructed the others, then jumped off the stage and from down on the dance floor hollered, "Let 'er rip!" If the crowd couldn't hear him from the stage he'd perform in their midst, with no microphone! He lit into "Whole lotta shakin' goin' on" and drew them like flies around dogshit, a logjam of couples pressing closer and closer to catch his voice, trying to jive to it. The musicians had to guess at their accompaniment. They didn't know where Sully was, he was lost in the throng, and they couldn't hear him. The dancers jostled to keep within his range, trying to catch the words above the noise from the stage, jiving wildly, bumping into him, elbowing, tramping on his feet, knocking him to his knees. He kept singing, flailing his arms to fend them off, spurred on by shouts of "Louder! We can't hear you!" — raising his voice, yelling the song at the top of his lungs —

Come along, baby!

We got shakin' in the barn —

By the time the song was over he was a mass of bruises — And they were still complaining, saying he hadn't sung loud enough —

"Fuck yez, then," he said. Most hadn't known he was singing at all, they thought it was just the band massacring another instrumental — nobody knew what it was supposed to be —

"Where'd you go to?" Harris said. "I thought you were gonna sing?"

"What do you think I was doing down there?"

"I couldn't hear you."

"Well, boys, I'm through for the night," said Ralph. He settled himself in his chair by the velveteen backdrop. "You guys go ahead without me. I've earned my five dollars. You don't need me."

"Play a waltz, William, something slow so they can dance," said Sully.

"What should I play?"

"Do 'All in the Game' — You can do that good—"

"I don't know that one," said Harris.

"You don't know your arse from your ear-hole," said Sully. "Sit this one out. And Nick, for Godsake, try it nice and soft for a change."

"Who do you think you are — Guy Lombardo? You ain't runnin' this band—"

"You can't use the fuckin' brushes anyway—"

"I can use them."

"Well, try it. See how it works."

After the infernal dissonance that'd gone before, William's solo number was nothing less than sublime. The girls on the committee stirred, they'd been skulking despondently in the corners, but now they looked at one another. Couples were actually up dancing, gravitating towards the stage where they could hear the piano —

Harris was refilling his 7-Up bottle with diluted vodka when Ellen Saunders marched through the stage door. He paused in his pouring. "What do you think, some good band, eh?" It all sounded great to Harris — with his ear. She gave him a disdainful glance and went over to Nick and Sully.

"We're having intermission in a few minutes," she said abruptly.

"We could use a break," said Sully.

"Then I want to talk to you."

"Go ahead. What's on your mind?"

"Not now. At intermission."

Another girl had trailed up onto the stage after her, a little thing with big ears named Myrna. She grinned, giving Sully the eye.

"We want to have a spot dance, and then there'll be a twenty minute break. William can play a waltz – just the piano–"

"Yeah, that'll be good, a spot dance, that'll make them happy," said Sully. "I'll announce it for you. Where's the spot gonna be?"

"You don't announce that."

"I know. You think I'm stupid?"

"We'll have to pick one." The two girls whispered together, looking out over the floor, pointing, shaking their heads, finally nodding in agreement.

"We have it now."

"You better explain to William how to do this. He probably doesn't know what a spot dance is."

Ellen went over to the piano, and Sully turned to the other girl. "Myrna, have a drink." He held his bottle out.

"Oh, I couldn't. Not here. Everyone can see us."

"Suit yourself. I'll have it for you."

"The chaperones are watching you guys."

"The hell with them."

She turned to leave.

"Save me a dance, will you?"

"I might." She grinned back at him.

"Hey – Where's the spot, anyway? I want to watch."

"Oh... Well, it's under the second light, over there to the right – the second from the stage. Don't tell anyone."

"What's the prize?"

"A pen set for the boy and earrings for the girl."

Everyone was dancing this one, hoping to win the prize – crowding towards the stage to be near the piano, butting into one another, shuffling this way and that trying to guess the spot. At Sully's suggestion I went down on the floor myself to get in on it.

"There's no room here," said Lois, the girl I asked to dance. "Everyone's bumping into us. Let's move over there."

"No, this is good enough. We can hear the music a little. It's the same everywhere."

Our feet were glued to the floor, we were hemmed in tightly, moving our knees in time with the music. William was playing "Love Letters in the Sand", playing it over and over again. Lois's cheek nestled against mine, the smell of her hair fresh in my nostrils, her hips swaying in slow rhythm as the piano played on – When the music came to a sudden stop everyone froze –

"Do you think we won?" said Lois.

There was a crepe ball suspended from the light overhead. I could reach up and touch it if I wanted –

I caught sight of Myrna making her way towards us, squeezing through the press of bodies, no one budging an inch for fear of moving off the spot. When she reached us she looked at me and at the light overhead and back at me again. "Oh no," she said. Having given away the location herself she was stuck.

"What is it? Did we win?" said Lois.

Myrna sighed – there wasn't much she could do – "I guess you're the winners."

"How about that!" I said.

We followed Myrna to the stage where she gave us our prizes. Then she announced in a deadpan voice the name of the lucky couple. There was a pause, then an enormous reaction from the floor, an uproarious protest –

"Robbery!"

"It was rigged!"

"Boooo!"

"Fixed!"

"Cheats!"

Lois's face was red. "Did you know all the time? "You crook! So that's why we stayed in that same place–"

It was a minute or two before Myrna could get across that it was now intermission time, with sandwiches and cakes available for everyone. When the message sank in the mob suddenly lost interest in the spot dance and thundered in a body towards the food table – it was everyone for himself –

Sully called me over. "Did you plant our sandwich?" he said.

"I couldn't." I told him about the girls keeping guard.

"Let me have it. I got an idea."
I retrieved the bag from its hiding place in the prop room and gave it to him. As we were leaving the stage he said over his shoulder, "Harris, do you want a sandwich?"

"Sure! Get me one, will you? But not egg."

"No, I'll get you something good."

I went ahead of him and got a paper plate from the table, and on the way back we transferred our sandwich onto it. "Wait here a few seconds so he don't suspect nothing," said Sully. "Let me handle it." When I reached them Harris was turning a section of the sandwich over and scrutinizing it from all angles. He said, "What kinda thing is this? Where'd you find it, in the garbage can?"

"Don't be so goddamn choosey. There's nothing wrong with it."

"Just look at it! Jesus, I ain't eatin' that. What's in it?" He sniffed at it. "Fuck! It smells like shit! I ain't eatin' this goddamn thing. Take it back. Throw it away."

"Let me see," I said. I held it near my nose — but not too close. "Nothing wrong with that. It smells good. Chicken salad, I think."

"You eat it, then."

"I already had one. I had one just like it."

"I'm throwing this sonuvawhore away."

"Don't — give it to me!" said Sully. "You can starve, then. Someone else'll eat it."

"I bet they will. I wonder who made that? Jesus Christ! I'd hate to eat at their house!"

"I'll get you another one, while I'm over there," said Sully, "if you're so jeezless particular. I'm going over again."

When I caught up to him he was already at the food table. One of the girls on guard had spotted him doing a switch. "No, but I made a mistake," he was explaining, "I thought this was a ham sandwich — I was looking for ham — I'm with the band, eh? — This one's chicken salad or something – I'll just put it back and try another kind. I can't stand chicken salad–"

The girl looked our sandwich over critically. "Are you sure you got that here, Sully?"

"Where in hell else'd I get it? I was just here a minute ago."

"There's something funny about this..." There was definitely something mangy and sinister-looking about our sandwich, especially alongside the others on the table... She picked up one of the quarters and examined it cautiously. "I think I'd better throw this away," she said.

"No, no, wait."

"Nobody's going to eat this–"

"Yes, they will. I think I'll have a piece of it myself, after all – just one – " He quickly plucked a section for the plate. "Looks fine to me – very good, I think." He added, "You shouldn't waste good food. Think of all the starving kids in China – they'd love to have it. You'd better leave it there, some hungry bastard might come along, it might be his favorite kind."

"I don't think anyone would eat that." Ignoring Sully's protests she took the remaining three quarters and with a distasteful expression on her lips dropped them in the scrap can.

Sully took another plate, piled it up, muttering "the goddamn cunt" and the like, and when we were back on the stage he handed the plate to Harris. "Now, don't complain. I'm not going back again. If you weren't so lazy you'd get your own."

"Thanks, Sully. I'll do something for you sometime."

We moved off to one side while Harris went at the food with an appetite, stuffing his face with both hands. Halfway through the pile his jaw suddenly locked – He looked closely at the half-eaten sandwich in his hand and at the stack still remaining on his plate. "Holy old – Sully, there's one of those others here!"

"Did you eat it?" Sully rushed over. "He ate it!"

"No, I didn't eat it. You think I'm crazy? It's right here." It was sitting on top of the remaining heap. He pointed at it. "I'm throwing this away – I bet you guys made this."

"You only got one left? I gave you two."

"Two?" Harris examined the uneaten sandwiches. He went pale.

"Yeah – You ate one, you stupid prick–"

"No, I didn't. I would've known – You cocksucker—"

Sully led me away, laughing loudly – "Aw, the hell with it. Next time we'll have to be more careful – so it don't look so shitty – That's what ruined it—"

Nick was calling us over to the drums –

"Them quiffs want us to quit," he said. "They want the fruit to play by himself. They don't like our music."

I'd caught a glimpse of Ellen Saunders and a couple of other girls talking to him – They were gone now –

"I told them it was a fuckin' insult, us drawing a crowd like this... They must've pulled in a hundred, two hundred dollars. I asked for half the gate – take it or leave it. Those are the terms. For a split of the gate we'll let William play – he can jerk off for an encore, for all I care. They were supposed to give us half the take anyway – But she forgot about that—"

"Where'd they go? What'd they say?"

"They wouldn't do it. I had to throw them off the stage. Fuck them. We'll play the way we want. We're doing okay – they just got no taste in music."

The intermission ran overtime – so much so that the crowd began to thin some – a sporadic drift towards the exit. The food was all gone and there were young drunks climbing up on the stage and mingling with the band – passing bottles around, staggering into each other, fiddling with the instruments, letting their girlfriends see they were friends with the musicians. For all anyone could tell the dance was over already. A couple of voices crowed from the floor – diehards who wanted more action, something for their money –

"Where's the music! We wanna dance!"

"We better get the second half going," said Nick. "Clear those young bastards off the stage. Get off the fuckin' stage!"

"I know what we can play," said Harris. "I just thought of it. 'Rebel Rouser'."

"We never practiced that one."

"Yeah, but I know it. I forgot all about it."

"Where's that jeezless Ramsay?"

Ralph was still sitting in his chair.

"Get up off your arse, Ralph, and earn your money – What do you think we hired you for?"

"You guys go ahead. I'll just sit here and listen."

"I'll play the trumpet," said Sully.

"You can't play that, Sully," said Ralph.

It was another ten minutes before the stage was cleared and they were in position. When the "music" started a few couples made a move to dance, when they saw the band was prepared to play — but they quickly thought better of it. Even William was out of the picture by this time. He wasn't accustomed to all this drinking. In the excitement he'd been taking repeated nips at his bottle, and there was always somebody filling it up for him. Dearborn nudged me, pointing at him. I watched his fingers run up the keyboard and off the end — he almost fell on his face — like someone had pulled the piano out from under him.

The Creatures poured it on mercilessly — Harris turned the amp up full force — he'd drunk all his diluted vodka and got into the real stuff. Sully blaring on the trumpet — hair-raising atonal blasts — they really did it up fine. Nick beating the drums to death. It was an appalling noise, atrocious, inhuman, the place like a madhouse, the sound accumulating and intensifying, bulging the walls. The crowd began rushing for the exit. It was as if somebody had yelled "Fire!"

"Let's get out of here," I called to Dearborn. It wasn't just the noise, it was the man with the white collar. There was a sudden backwash at the exit, the stampede faltering, subsiding, spreading back in over the floor again. I hollered for the band to stop but they couldn't possibly hear me. Sully shrugged me aside when I tugged at his sleeve. I exited stage-left and got in among the crowd, with Dearborn behind me. He'd seen the priest coming too — saw him crossing the floor, and now bounding up the steps at the side and standing by the amplifier waving his arms wildly, trying to still the inferno—

Sully suddenly thrust the trumpet into Ralph's lap. The guitar ceased, Harris taking in who the man was in front of him. Then the drums. The piano carried on by itself, William with his back turned, pounding the keys for all he was worth—

"I said STOP!"

"Oh!" William jumped and swivelled unsteadily around on his stool. His rapt smile faded as the image of the priest came into focus.

There was almost total silence in the hall, and for a moment Father Malley said nothing; he was trembling, trying to maintain control of himself, conscious of his dignity. He stared at The Creatures one by one.

"This — this is an *outrage*," he said at last. "If I'd had any idea such a performance would take place in a Catholic school — " His voice shook — "Why, you're all drunk, I can see it — " His eyes fastened on William. "And you, William Bryenton — of all people—"

"Oh golly — I — I didn't mean anything, Father—"

"In a Catholic school! What is the meaning of all this? If I'd had any idea — " He turned to Ralph who was sitting motionless with his elbows on his knees, eyes averted, staring at the backdrop, as though he wasn't there at all.

"Imagine! A man your age! What sort of example is this to set? You should be ashamed of yourself. What's in that bottle?"

"Hello, Father."

Without looking at him Ralph held the bottle up before his eyes. "It says ginger ale on the label. It must be ginger ale, Father —"

"Hm! Yes, I'm sure! Have you no shame? This sort of thing will never happen again. There'll be no more of these dances. I was afraid this would happen — None of you is fit to be trusted — If I'd known—"

"Hm, God... The Lord says..." The priest whipped around. It was Sully, imitating his voice, the way Father Malley delivered his sermons, with a self-important nasal intonation. Sully looked over his shoulder, as though the guilty party were behind him. "How's it going, anyway, Father?" he said.

"*You* — I'm not surprised to see *you* here — When they told me — " He sputtered, then stopped short, aware that hundreds of eyes were on him. He was rescued from an exchange with Sully — who was bad enough sober — when Nick all of a sudden threw back his head and began draining his bottle for fear the booze would be confiscated. You could hear the liquid bubbling down his throat, his adam's apple bobbing. The priest was aghast. He jumped in the air with exasperation. "Stop that!" Nick took it to the last drop and placed the empty on the floor beside him. His throat was hoarse from the raw liquor, his eyes shining. "Only pop, Father," he whispered, coughing. He exhaled loudly. "Whew!" There were empty pints lying all over the stage. They'd become careless at intermission, with so many guys roaming about the stage, passing drinks every which way — discarding empties — It was obviously time for a level head to step in and clear the air. Harris planted himself in front of the priest — He had everything under control, he assured Father Malley. The boys meant no harm, it was all the fault of the microphone not working – The priest cut him short – "I don't want to hear another word." He brushed him aside and stepped to the lip of the stage and informed the crowd that they could all go home, the dance was over. "And you needn't expect there'll be another one. I won't have a repeat of this disgusting spectacle!" Turning back to The Creatures he said, "The sooner you're out of here the better."

"Hm, Jesus, Father..." Sully mocking him again, doing his voice. The priest was livid with indignation. He opened his mouth, then thought better of it, rounded on his heel and walked off the stage. A path opened for him and he strode out the door.

The auditorium came to life then, everyone talking at once –

"One minute, please! Before you all leave!" Ellen Saunders stood on the stage now, screaming. "Listen to me! You saw what happened – You all saw it – We were going to have these dances every Friday night – but now that's been ruined!"

"She's the one ratted on us," said Nick.

"We won't be able to have any more dances! You know whose fault it is! You know who's responsible – I hope some of you see they get what's coming to them – They need to be taught a lesson! – They've ruined it for everybody! We could've had these dances every week – Father Malley said we could – And now we can't – " She went on like this for several minutes, her fury increasing, her words becoming less coherent and more repetitive – raving –

People began to drift towards the exit. From behind her Nick squawked, "Sit down, you silly cunt!"

That only caused her to scream louder — denouncing the band — trying to inspire the crowd to massacre them — revenge themselves — revenge everyone — the CY-High — the committee — Father Malley — the Catholic Church! One of the drunks near the exit hollered, "Speech over!" and another followed with,"Let's get the hell out of here!"

"That was great music, boys!" Drunken laughter.

The movement towards the exit was contagious and she was forced at last to stop ranting. She was only embarrassing herself, losing her temper like that. Nobody cared, they'd had their entertainment. it was all worth the price of admission. The arrival of the priest had put the icing on the cake. Everyone was satisfied.

Before too long they were all gone, the auditorium deserted, just the band there, in no rush to leave, and a couple of the committee girls at the ticket table waiting impatiently to lock up and go home — casting hostile looks up at the stage —

§

And that was it.

They dropped me off sometime around three in the morning, all of us drunk as owls, and I seem to recall they were going home themselves; but they didn't, they drove to Clifton for a last little run, and on the way back smashed head-on into a hydro pole. The type of thing you read about in the papers every day or so. Nick was banged up enough to make the critical list, a fractured skull, half a dozen broken ribs, a broken leg, some internal injuries – odds and ends of things – but he was as good as new in a few months. When you saw the wreck it seemed impossible but Harris had crawled out without a scratch – And Sully – that was the end of him – here one day and gone the next –

EPILOGUE

I SAW RALPH THE LAST time I was home, this past summer, fifteen years after the debut and demise of The Creatures. He was living in a different place, in a little house that he'd inherited when his mother and father died, within months of each other. There wasn't much noticeable change in him, he hardly looked a day older. He happened to be on the wagon just then. He told me he stayed in the house most of the time these days.

"I never feel like going out. I sit in here and look at Playboy magazine, that's about all I do. I go to bed every night with Playboy magazine. What an imagination! I've got more girlfriends than I can handle. I said to a girl once that I was just the fellow she was looking for. I said Manpower had sent me – I said I had the manpower – and she says, 'Manpower? You mean handpower! You don't mean manpower, you mean handpower.' Holy sufferin'..."

When I mentioned the night he played for the dance he said, "Don't remind me. I'd forgotten all about it. Father what's-his-name... Malley. 'You're giving these kids ideas,' he says to me. 'You should be ashamed of yourself.' Giving them ideas — that was a good one. It should have been the other way around. They were the ones got me there, they had all the booze."

"How's William doing? What's he up to these days?"

"I don't know, I haven't seen him in years. He joined the priests after he finished college. He's in Ontario somewhere, I think."

"And Nick? How's he making out?"

"Oh, he's just the same. He's driving a taxi and bootlegging. He's got five or six kids. I see him around. He's still the same. Guys never change, it's only women who change. They pull out their eyebrows, dye their hair, put on make-up. You can't hardly tell who they are from one day to the next... Harris was telling me a few weeks ago that he can do anything I can do, bragging like that. I've been off the bottle close to two months now. I said to him, try that for a start. So he tried and he lasted two days before he was drunk again. It's not easy. A lot of people think it's easy. Maybe it is for other people, but Harris couldn't do it. He's always coming around — he's been company, but he gets too drunk, so I don't want to see him anymore — not when he's drunk all the time —

"I go down to the AA's now. But it's harder for me than the others, being alone the way I am. There's only two of us down there not married and it's a lot tougher that way, nobody to encourage you along, to help you keep going. I think of having a drink all the time, but shit, I don't want to kill myself, that's what I was doing... All the same, I don't feel any better now, I still don't feel good. But that's what they tell you — don't expect us to make you feel good, all we can do is get you to stop drinking. It doesn't mean you'll be happy once you've stopped, at least not right away... maybe eventually, but I don't know... they say it gets better...

"The crowd I was hanging around with, a lot of them, I don't want to have any more to do with that bunch... They argue and fight, they never sit down and have a peaceful conversation or a song or a little music. They get drunk and all they want to do is fight. They start wrist wrestling, that kind of stuff. I hate that. The next thing you know they're fighting, they all want to show how tough and strong they are, and how smart they are, they know everything... but they don't know anything at all, just stupid arguing. And they get spewing all over the place, throwing up on the floor and the furniture. I've had enough of that. I said no more of it. Someone even stole my boots. That's what it was like. One night a gang of them were here, all those winos, and when they left my boots were gone — I don't think they walked out by themselves. At least I didn't see them walking out... Maybe they did...

"I wrote to these invention people. They like one of my inventions... They even phoned me from New York. That's something, eh? I said to the guy, 'How's everyone in New York?' He says, 'How should I know, I don't have time to go around asking everyone in New York how they are.' 'How's everyone in New York!' Imagine saying that? He's paying for a long distance call and I ask him how everyone is in New York. He tells me he has a penthouse there. I said to him, 'Is that right? I've got a henhouse here too.' They must've thought, what kind of crazy character is this? A mad inventor — from the backwoods of New Brunswick. Talking crazy like that, them paying for a long distance phone call and me talking that kind of foolishness... They told me I didn't have to pay for the search fee all at once, I can pay it in monthly installments, twenty-five dollars a month. I wrote them before, telling them I was having some financial problems... but I guess I can borrow twenty-five dollars a month... I don't know. I'm not a fool, I don't want to get stuck for something, they could be making a sucker out of me. It'd cost seven hundred and fifty in the end, once I got started... A hundred and fifty for the search... Maybe I could sell the idea once I knew it was original, that it was mine and nobody else had registered the same thing. I could let some company pay for the patent. I guess that's what I'll do. Carl McGuire said he'd help me anytime, I think he'll give me twenty-five dollars. He'd have given me more if they'd won the election. He was running for the Liberals. I worked for him, you know, lugging a ladder all over town putting up posters. Someone asked me why I didn't run myself. I said run? I can hardly walk, carrying this damn ladder all over the place. Carl said if half the workers had done as much as me the party would be in today. He's in himself but the party lost. He'll lend me twenty-five dollars, I think. Maybe he will. I'll ask him. They'll want me to work the next election...

"I'm going to try to keep sober for a year, if I can. Take it one day at a time, that's the way you're supposed to do it. And then maybe I'll be able to have a drink sensibly, keep a bottle around and have a little now and then and not go and drink it all at once. I think I could do that. Other people do it, no reason why I can't. I'm not that much different. I'm pretty sure I'm a human like everyone else."

Raymond Fraser is the author of twelve books of fiction, three of non-fiction, and six collections of poetry. His novel *The Bannonbridge Musicians* was runner-up for the Governor General's Award in 1978. In 2009 following publication of his novel *In Another Life* he received the Lieutenant-Governor's Award for High Achievement in the Literary Arts. He was appointed to the Order of New Brunswick in 2012 for his contributions to literature and culture in the province.
http://raymondfraser.blogspot.com

www.ingramcontent.com/pod-product-compliance
Lightning Source LLC
Chambersburg PA
CBHW030902060726
47591CB00005B/1382